The Painting 3

By Kathleen J. Shields

This book is a work of fiction. Places, events, and situations in this story are purely fictional. Any resemblance to actual persons, living or dead, is coincidental.

ISBN-13:   978-1-941345-47-4 Paperback

ISBN-E: 978-0-463855-60-7 Smashwords

ERIN GO BRAGH *Publishing*

Canyon Lake, TX
www.ErinGoBraghPublishing.com

Foreword

Imagination is key...

The human brain is capable of the most complex manifestations of intelligence ever imaginable. Not only is the brain responsible for every single action, movement, breath or step we make, it is also credited with every innovation humankind has ever created.

When there is a need, the brain discovers a way. With our imagination we are able to produce and simulate complex thoughts and memories into our senses and form an understanding in our mind. This can turn past experiences and lessons into more, by completely inventing new and ingenious ways to solve problems.

We take the basic training our lives have given us to open up possibilities to better our situations or the lives of those around us. It was the imagination that honed electricity, designed the car, and discovered a way to record our stories onto film. The imagination brought us the understanding of fire and the warmth it gave, the intelligence to sow the seeds of the foods we wanted to grow and the knowledge of medical advancements that can cure the sick and vaccinate us from diseases.

Every great innovation through time came from a spark of imagination. The inventor saw a need, realized a solution and created a way to make it happen. Imagination is the spirit and tenacity that leads to progress.

We were born with a brain capable of learning, growing and expanding our understanding so we could imagine greatness, to interpret the world around us and envision ways to make it better.

Our imagination is our greatest gift, the most important aspect of humanity. It must be cultivated, cherished and encouraged – so we can further ourselves and each other.

Chapter 1

Desire is a sense of longing, a hope for a better outcome.
It is a thought that flows out of one person and becomes
something real. Desire is what makes plans succeed.
It comes from the heart. Desire takes faith.

- K

The Painting was flourishing as were its people. Gerald had painted a perfect world, a masterpiece so awesome, it came to life. A world so amazing, he had to perform the miraculous to protect it. Then, when it was time, he sent his son, Benjamin, into the Painting in order to teach the people about his father, the one who painted them. You would have thought the story was complete, but Gerald knew there was one more thing needed.

When Benjamin returned home, he experienced conflicting emotions. He had lived two lives – one growing up with his father, the painter of a universe. A life that taught him about the joys of doing good, the perils of bad and the incredible opportunities his father granted for those people within the Painting.

His second life was designed so he would utilize the knowledge his father had bestowed upon him growing up, in order to share it with the inhabitants of the Painting. He was born there, grew up and lived within the Painting. He died in the Painting. His second life was enchanting, beautiful and traumatic. He witnessed first-hand the miracles of his father's world, his influences and how wonderful life could be, if only they would let it.

He had an understanding greater than any could possibly comprehend, and a message that was so valiant it strengthened fear within those who couldn't understand.

When he returned, he, too, heard the people of the Painting, just like his father. He heard their joy, laughter and excitement. He also heard their cries, conflicts and sadness. He felt the pain they felt, and the hurt it left in his heart was powerful.

It took him quite a long time to adapt to the changes in his life – but adapt he did. With the overwhelming assortment of emotions barraging him day-in and day-out, he decided he had to go to his father for help.

"Father, I've seen you, and watched you for years. I know you hear and feel this, and I've seen what it can do to you. But I've also seen you at peace. I've seen you where the accumulation of cries didn't overwhelm you. Father, I need to know how you do it."

"You need to find your own inner joy, son. You need to discover something in your life that brings you peace and tranquility."

With some soul searching, Benjamin realized his dream of painting – to be like his father. He would paint scenes from his father's world, like beautiful pastures of flowing green grasses swaying in the breeze and colorful sunsets shimmering into still waters, mirroring the beauty and doubling the majesty of the scene.

He'd paint flowers and birds, so many landscapes, an array of settings that had brought him joy. Seascapes of crashing waves on shimmering rocks, a multitude of blues and greens mixed with pristine whites that according to the hues of paint shouldn't be possible.

His father adored his son's work, but he knew that painting wasn't the only thing his son needed in order to find peace. He encouraged his son to venture out, to explore the world he had long forgotten *their* world.

So Benjamin did. He ventured out into their world and discovered all that he had been missing. Of course, compared to the Painting,

Benjamin found himself unimpressed. Within the Painting he had seen anger, confusion, hate and mistrust – but he had also experienced love, friendship, and compassion. As he ventured throughout his world he found increasing disappointment, loneliness. He felt as if he didn't belong here.

"Father, I'm suffering. I feel so alone and lost. I want to go back, but I'm afraid. I want to stay here but I feel unwelcome. I don't know what to do with these emotions."

"Find someone to share them with."

Benjamin walked away feeling conflicted. That's what he had tried to do with his father, and he was dismissed. Why? He was sitting on a bench mulling this over when a woman sat down beside him. Why she sat down next to him wasn't important, why she decided to strike up a conversation with him wasn't the point. The fact that she listened, cared and heard him, that's what mattered.

She understood him. They discovered commonality, they melded and became friends.

This friend, with her bright smile and keen intellect, her appreciation of his talents, who devoted herself to him, also became his wife. And after some time, he was gifted with a child of his very own. The day he presented his newborn daughter to his father was one of the happiest and joyous of Benjamin's life.

"Her name is Nevaeh." *(Neh-Vay-Uh)*

"A perfect name for a truly perfect being." Gerald smiled knowingly. "I am so happy for you, my son."

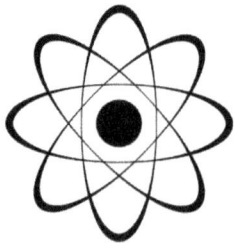

Chapter 2

Now that Benjamin was a father, he developed so much more appreciation for what his own father had done for him. He understood the pride and fear of being wholly responsible for this tiny soul. He worried for her, protected her, and would do anything for her. He wanted for nothing but her happiness, for her to be safe, and then it occurred to him what his father must have gone through with him.

Letting him go into the Painting must have been the most terrifying decision he had ever made. Knowing what was going to happen, letting go of his hold, his protection of his son. Benjamin thought about his own daughter and how devastating it would be to his heart to see her hurt, even for a minute. But then he realized why. The Painting was his legacy. His father's creation was his undertaking. His assignment was to share love. It was the same expression as the love he felt for his own daughter.

Raising this precious life showed him how frail we all are. Benjamin realized how closely related the emotion of love and fear are. He understood how easily the conflict could escalate, how quickly the emotions could flip. He had seen and shared the beauty of his father's design, but he hadn't understood the passion until now.

Benjamin had been sure he had shared his father's love with the Painting, but now he wondered had he really? He knew there were many who declared Geody's love, who shared with others the beauty of what they had learned, but there was still division. There were still people who were afraid, angry, confused. It was they who had expelled Benjamin from the Painting with their fears, their anger, their absence of connection, and their lack of love.

Benjamin realized he had failed them. Had he failed his father, too?

Sitting with him in his study, Benjamin watched his father stare at the Universe Painting. His eyes glistened as he followed the stars spiral around the sun. He heard the laughter and cries of the people within, his heart ached for them.

"Father, I think I failed you."

Gerald turned to his son in confusion, "How could you think that?"

"I only touched half of the people. There is such division, so much conflict and confusion scattered throughout your Painting."

"You know you did everything I wanted of you, and then some. I am so proud of the work you did. Don't ever think I'm not."

"I thought I knew everything about life. I thought I had learned everything there was to learn. I have literally lived two lives, how could I have not known?" Benjamin declared.

"Because there is more to life than simply living." Gerald spoke as he stood from his chair. "Take a look at this Painting, what do you see?"

Benjamin stood and looked, but before he could come up with an answer, his father spoke.

"I see infinite possibilities for everyone, and an inexhaustible array of opportunities for an immeasurable amount of people. And every single one of those options are connected to the life experiences of that particular person at that precise moment in their existence. The same exact advantage for one could be a dilemma for another. It's all about perspective. Your perspective was that of a son, there was absolutely nothing wrong with what you did, just like no one in the Painting could make the wrong choice, if their heart's choice is pure."

"So how can we change the hearts of those who don't understand?"

"That opportunity will come in time. I didn't paint this canvas in a day, so you can't expect the answer to evolve overnight."

Benjamin nodded and they both stood in silence for a long moment.

"Dada, what are you and Grampa doing?"

They both turned to see little Nevaeh standing at the door. They smiled at her and then glanced at each other.

"Come here, Sweetheart. Do you want to see something neat?" She walked over to them, and Benjamin lifted her into his arms. He braced her on his hip and pointed her attention to the Painting. "Your Grandfather painted this."

Nevaeh gazed at the Painting and realized it was moving. Her eyes widened as she marveled at the canvas. She touched it, the rough canvas, feeling the texture on her finger tips and yet the landscape moved. She followed the stars as they spun around the sun. And she giggled as she traced her finger following the motion of the planets.

The three of them sat down and regaled the young girl with fascinating stories of a Painting come to life, and a world of magical hope and of a beauty unlike any she had ever seen. The stories fascinated Nevaeh, her mind reeled with questions, a desire to hear more stories, and so they shared until she couldn't keep her eyes open any longer.

From then on, whenever they'd visit her grandfather, Gerald, he would show her the majesty of the universe Painting and enthrall her with stories of the original Painting within. He'd tell her all about how he could step inside of the Painting, as if walking through a door. He told her about the fluffy white bunny whose whiskers tickled his nose, and how the sunset would paint the sky in the most beautiful colors imaginable.

Then when she'd go home, she'd ask her father, Benjamin, to tell her more stories about his growing up within the Painting. He showed her his artwork, all of the beautiful scenes he had painted from memory, and she loved them.

Yet, while Nevaeh loved the stories, she was filled with confusion. All she ever saw was the stars. She watched how the stars and planets spiraled around the sun in an awe-inspiring display of color and energy, but she couldn't seem to understand how this dark canvas of white specs spinning like a top, held within it such an amazing world. Until she understood, she was determined to watch it.

As a toddler, Nevaeh's eyes would glisten as she stared at the dazzling painting hanging on the wall in her grandfather's study. She'd lie in his lap and simply stare at it while he rocked her to sleep. Then she would dream about seeing all of the sights she heard about.

As she grew, she began exploring, walking and choosing which rooms she wanted to visit. Time and time again she'd return to her grandfather's study where they'd later find her sitting on the floor staring up at the Painting.

They declared that they had been looking for her, and she'd sweetly turn to them with a smile and ask, "Where else would I be?"

When she turned old enough, Gerald did something Benjamin couldn't even comprehend – he gave Nevaeh the Painting.

"What?" Benjamin nearly collapsed from the shock. "You are giving her the Painting?"

"I am."

Benjamin's head was reeling. His father had always had the Painting. It hung on the wall of his study his entire life. Why now, after all of this time, after everything this painting meant to him and to Benjamin, would he give it to a young girl?

"Nevaeh has heard the stories. We've both shared with her the enchantment of a world she can't see, and she's been taught by the most amazing father I have ever met." Gerald smiled at Benjamin. "My son, it is nearing her time. It is time for this Painting to hang on her wall, so she can marvel at it as you did growing up."

Benjamin looked quizzically at his father, then at the Painting. "I remember growing up, sitting in this den watching the Painting for hours. I remember asking you questions about it, questions that occurred to me after long stents of time wondering about it curiously."

"And that, my son, is why she should have it on her wall – in *your* house."

"But why our house? How could you part with something so precious?"

"What could be more precious than you?"

"Won't you miss it?"

"I could never miss anything that stays with me, heart and soul."

Maybe we should hang it in our living room, or my studio?"

"How much time does she spend in those rooms, son? Would she get the full benefit of viewing it there?"

"No, I guess not." Benjamin hummed, "But Father, I wouldn't want it to get ruined. What if she spills something on it, or draws on it?"

Gerald smiled. "What could she do to a universe so dense and black that wouldn't make it become something better?"

Benjamin shrugged his shoulders. By the end of the day Nevaeh was sitting on the edge of her bed staring at the most magnificent Painting in the cosmos. While Benjamin worried a little bit, he trusted his father.

Chapter 3

It had been a week of Nevaeh asking many questions, some of which caught Benjamin completely by surprise. He was quite impressed with his inquisitive little girl. He was talking with his wife about her latest question when he heard Nevaeh calling them from upstairs. "Daddy, Daddy, come see!" They ran up the stairs and into her room to witness what Benjamin feared most.

"Father, you need to come over, now." Benjamin spoke into the phone.

"Why? What's going on?"

"I can't tell you over the phone. This is something you need to see in person."

"Okay Son, I'll be over in a bit."

About twenty minutes later Gerald arrived. He was walked upstairs in silence.

"What's going on? Why all the secrecy?"

"There you go." Benjamin spoke low as he pointed to the Painting hanging on the wall in Nevaeh's room.

"Isn't it amazing?" Nevaeh smiled as bright as the sun shining in the Painting. She leapt on her bed joyfully.

Gerald peered over at the Painting and smirked with delight. "It truly is."

"Father, you can't be serious!" Benjamin croaked. But Gerald held up a finger.

Benjamin watched as his father the creator of this universe, approached the

Painting hanging on the wall and carefully examined the newly added splotches.

"May I make one little alteration?" Gerald asked of Nevaeh who was so proud of her vibrantly colorful watercolor addition. She nodded her head.

"Come closer." He spoke as he pulled out a chair from under her desk. Nevaeh hopped down off her bed, skipped over to her grandfather, and climbed onto the chair.

"Watch this." He spoke whimsically as he pressed his palm over one of the splotches, closed his eyes, and pressed on it as if he were pushing something heavy through a tiny hole.

When he removed his hand, Nevaeh clapped proudly as she took in the most amazing magical feat she had ever seen. Gerald had taken her splotch of orange and blue watercolor and pressed it into the Painting. It suddenly seemed so far away as it moved with the stars of the universe. What would someday be known as a nebula, a colorful cloud in a distant part of the universe, had been added by a child, and brought to life by Gerald.

"It looks like a giant eye ball!" Nevaeh screeched gleefully as she pointed at the now distant, spiraling splotch within the Painting.

"That is the blue part of the eyeball..."

"The Iris" Gerald assisted.

"And that looks like the skin around it."

Benjamin walked up closer to see. He was mystified – although he should have known better than to doubt his father, he still found himself astounded.

Just then Nevaeh leapt off of the chair, grabbed her watercolors and hopped back on the chair. She slapped her tiny palm into the colors and smeared some bluish purple in the bottom corner of the canvas. Then she smeared some orange-ish red to the right of the blue-green and made it look like it was swirling.

Then she wiped her hands on her apron and dabbed it in some pink. Tip-toeing on the chair, she reached up high and spread a wavy line across the top of the Painting. Then she grabbed her paintbrush and smeared a bit of light green just above it – it was a bold and stark contrast to the black space with white specs.

Looking at the lower corner she smeared a cloud of blue, then topped it with a swish of her paintbrush. Gerald stepped back and watched as Nevaeh embellished his masterpiece with her creative style, with her joy of colors, with her youthful innocence, and he marveled at it. He was so proud of her when she turned to him and exclaimed – "Now, do it again!"

Gerald stepped up to her, cupped his palm over a blob of color and pressed it into the painting. When he removed his hand and Nevaeh saw what he had done she squealed with delight. "Again!"

Gerald did it again, and again, pressing all of the unique blotches, splashes, splotches, dabs and blots into the universe and setting them in motion around the sun. The colors followed the stars. They swirled and mixed within the universe until there was an expanse of colorful reminders that something bigger and better was out there.

"What a splendid imagination you have, Nevaeh. How did you realize that this Painting would benefit from a splash of color?"

"Color is the most precious gift we have. There are so many kinds of colors - so many reds and yellows and greens and purples that there is almost no way that you can mix a palette and ever get the same exact color twice."

"That's very true." Benjamin chimed in, marveling at his daughter's insight.

Chapter 4

"That looks like a butterfly. And that looks like a beach!" Nevaeh was saying as she pointed out the colorful blotches as they spiraled around the sun. "Aren't those the prettiest reds and pinks you've ever seen? Look how they sparkle!" She squealed with delight.

"And those purples and blues really help to brighten up that darker corner of space, don't you think?" Benjamin spoke, as his father and he stood at the doorway marveling at the newly revised masterpiece.

"Wait!" Nevaeh spoke as she leaped off her bed. She ran to the Painting and pointed at a spot that was coming around the sun that didn't have enough color. We need something there."

"Are you sure?" Gerald asked as he stepped up to the Painting to inspect the empty black area.

"Yeah, but it spins around so fast I'll never get to paint it, and have you press it inside, in time – what do we do?"

"I'll teach you how to do it, yourself."

"You will?" Excitement gleamed in her eyes.

"Of course. Did you not know that you have the gift?" He smiled.

"The gift?"

"Yes ma'am. I painted it. Your father was born into it, and you have the gift to see inside of it anytime you want."

"Really?" Her eyes sparkled with wonder and fascination.

"You have the ability to enact change. Whenever you want to do something for the good of it, you will be able to do it."

"Wow! How does it work?" Nevaeh clapped while jumping up and down, gleefully.

"It will take a while to learn, of course, but I can show you this one little trick right now. Would you like to learn?"

"Yes! Yes Grampa, I would!" Nevaeh squealed with delight as Benjamin glanced over to his wife, whose inquisitive look spoke volumes.

She had heard about Benjamin's adventure. She had a hard time truly believing it, but she acknowledged it as truth. Then, after she saw the Painting, the universe moving within a textured canvas, she accepted it even more. But she had also experienced Benjamin's mood swings, his sadness, his pain. She had seen residual memories attack him while he slept at night, awaking in fear. She knew how he died in the Painting, so hearing Gerald speak of Nevaeh's ability, made her panic inside.

"Okay," he clapped, "go get your paints." He watched her run to her desk, pick up her paints and paintbrush and then look up at him adoringly, awaiting instruction.

"Now paint the shape and color you want to create, on the palm of your hand."

She did so, carefully working out splotchy details, and then proudly held up her palm to show her grandfather.

"Oh, that is going to look nice." He turned back to the Painting, "Now, come here."

She leaped onto her chair and spotted the area she wanted to color. "Right there."

"Right here?" Gerald asked, making sure.

"Yes!"

"Okay. Hover your palm just above the canvas in that exact spot that you want this paint to appear." She did. "Now, think about it being right there, inside the Painting. Imagine the universe full of color in that exact spot.

Imagine how beautiful it would be, as you watch it spin around the universe, and then desire it."

"Desire? What's that?"

"Desire is having a feeling, a want, so strong, that you will do anything to make it happen. When YOU desire something, your sense of seeing your desire happen is excited by the enjoyment that you expect to feel when that item or person decides to take actions to obtain your goal. All you need to do is want it to happen strong enough, and it will happen. Can you do that?"

"I think so."

"Now visualize your splotch of color floating like a cloud in that dark, empty spot of space. See it spiraling around the sun, shimmering with the stars and becoming real. And when you have that vision, that desire in your mind, press your palm onto the Painting and push that paint right through the canvas."

Nevaeh looked at the Painting one more time. She spotted that dark spot one more time, then she closed her eyes envisioning that spot filling with the spiral colors on her hand. She saw them in her mind forming the nebula. When she had the perfect feeling of it, she pressed her palm onto the Painting, held it there for a few moments, willing it to work, and then pulled her hand away.

Benjamin was in awe. It had worked. When Nevaeh's eyes opened and she saw what she had done, she squealed in pure merriment.

"I did it! I did it! I did it!"

"Yes, you did." Gerald took the happy young girl into his arms and hugged her. "You can do anything YOU put your mind to!"

Chapter 5

That evening after dinner, after her grandparents left, Nevaeh returned back to her room to watch the Painting. A few hours later, Benjamin went upstairs to check on her and tuck her into bed.

"Daddy, tell me about the Painting?"

"What do you want to know?"

"Everything!"

"I've told you so much already…"

"But now, now I want every single detail."

So Benjamin refreshed her memory on how the Painting came to be. How her grandfather, Gerald, painted the world that came to life. How later he realized he needed to protect that world with everything he had in him, so he painted the universe. Then he explained how the Painting was pressed inside the universe, just like she pressed the colors inside today. Then he started it spinning around the brilliant, bright sun.

"And then you went into the Painting."

"That's correct. I was born into it. I grew up seeing so many fascinating, magnificent creations. The Painting is a marvelous place. The trees are exquisite, with so much detail you can hardly imagine. The flowers - you love colors – there are so many colors of flowers that dot the landscape. And the sunsets... to see a sunset again, to sit there and watch it dip down below the horizon, letting that explosion of color paint the sky with such beauty...." Benjamin trailed off simply reminiscing about it.

"I want to see it someday."

Benjamin pulled back from his memory and looked at his precious daughter sitting beside him, staring longingly at the Painting. He suddenly thought about his last day there, the explosion, the pain. He couldn't fathom a single thought of his daughter feeling that.

"I've painted them." He reminded her, "You've seen my paintings in my study."

"I have." She smiled.

If you ever want to see anything, I can always try to paint it for you."

That evening as Nevaeh lay in her bed, head on her pillow, she watched the Painting. The stars within shimmered like tiny diamonds. The new colors glowed with a radiance that entranced her senses. As her eyelids became heavy, she thought about flying into the Painting. She wondered how small she would be as she soared into each nebula. She wondered if the paint of the nebula would still be wet or if it would have dried by now. She wondered how close she could get to the stars. Could she touch them? Would they be cold or hot, smooth or sharp? And as her eyes closed, her mind drifted into the Painting.

When she awoke the next morning she was exhilarated. She leaped from her bed and ran downstairs. "Guess what!"

"What?" Her mother and Benjamin asked.

"I saw the stars!"

"That's nice dear." Her mother cooed.

"I saw the stars and they were huge! They were much bigger than I could have ever imagined. The nebulas were made of so many colors, and they were like massive clouds. I could soar through them but not really touch them. I was floating inside them, but not getting covered in paint. It was the most amazing adventure I've ever had!"

"That sounds like a wonderful dream, Sweetheart." Benjamin heard his wife say, but he grew ever more curious. When it came to his father's artwork, anything was possible.

"You should tell your grandfather about that! He would love to hear about it."

Later that day, Nevaeh relayed her experience all over again to Gerald. She held her arms out to the side and danced around her room, showing him how she flew through the colorful clouds in the dark black sky. She described how the stars drummed, and how she could hear them pulsate. Benjamin hadn't heard that part, where did that come from?

Gerald sat down with her and began asking so many questions. "How far did you go? What else did you see?"

"I flew for hours. I saw tiny planets and large planets. I saw one so big I couldn't see the entire thing with my eyes. But I was so far away from the sun."

"Was it cold?"

"I didn't feel cold."

"Did you smell anything?"

"No."

"Taste anything?"

"No." Nevaeh looked at him curiously.

"You just saw and heard the sights and sounds," he confirmed. Nevaeh nodded her head. "Wonderful." Gerald grinned.

"How is that wonderful?" Benjamin asked hanging on his father's every word.

"It's exactly how I imagined it would be." He paused forming his next words carefully. "Nevaeh, did you know that each time you fly into the Painting you can fly faster?"

"How do you mean?"

"Well, everything you've seen, you can soar past faster, if you want to. That way you can see what you haven't seen yet."

"I can go farther? Towards the sun?"

"Towards my Painting." Gerald declared. "That blue and green spinning spec, right there." He pointed to the twirling ball rotating around the sun, the marble that shimmered like an emerald.

"Oh, I want to go there!"

"Why?" Benjamin found the word escape his mouth before thinking.

"So I can see the world that my daddy lived in!" Nevaeh answered with adoration. "I want to see the trees and flowers. I want to watch the sunsets and hear the rain…"

Benjamin looked worried. His father took his hand and let Nevaeh finish her speech.

"I want to see the ocean and feel the fluffy white bunny tickle my nose with its whiskers!"

"Now that part can't happen." Gerald confirmed, intriguing even his son.

"Why?" Nevaeh asked with a tear forming in her eye. The disappointment apparent.

"Because you'd only be there in spirit."

"What does that mean?"

"It means you won't be able to touch anything. You won't feel cold or hot..."

Benjamin watched the excitement lift from his daughter's face, so he spoke up. "So you won't get burned or hurt."

"That's right." Gerald added. "You can't get pricked by a rose's thorn, scraped if you fall, or harmed in any way."

"That's good." Nevaeh smiled, but then the smile faded. "But I won't be able to feel the soft bunny's fur, or pet a deer..."

"True," Gerald acknowledged, then added, "but you'll be able to talk to them!"

"I will?" Her eyes beamed brightly.

"The animals of my world will be able to sense you. There are so many animals, so many species. Some will be able to feel your presence, you may catch them turn and look at you, maybe even look through you, as if they know you are there but can't see you. Others will be able to hear and see you. They may or may not interact with you, as some of my animals can be quite afraid of humans, but they may hear you. Wouldn't that be nice?"

"That really would be neat!" Nevaeh expressed with the brightest smile Benjamin had ever seen. "I can't wait to go there!"

Benjamin interjected. "But there is so much to see before you get there. I've seen some of it."

"I'll bet just looking at the Painting, your grandfather's world from above it in space would be amazing."

"I'll bet it would."

"You should spend plenty of time just experiencing all of the beautiful nature your grandfather has painted when you get there."

"Like what?"

"Like the plants, the trees, the ocean. There is so much to see, it may take you years!"

"Wow!" Nevaeh cooed.

"Spend as much time as you can seeing the world, the land, the seas, the mountains…"

"I will, Daddy."

Gerald glanced over sadly at his son. He understood Benjamin's worry, he knew of his son's fear, but he was certain Nevaeh would be safe. He just wished he could confirm that with his son. Time would tell.

Chapter 6

Over the course of many weeks Nevaeh explored the universe. She flew farther - farther into the Painting, seeing sights no one had ever imagined. As she neared the original Painting, Gerald's world, she couldn't help but stop and hover above it. It was the most outstanding sight she had ever seen, and up until now, she had seen some pretty amazing sights!

The simplicity of the clouds, flowing around the planet, the fluffy white, the heavy grey, and the lightning... the lightning alone was magnificent! The wiry lines, jagged rays of light spider webbing across the sky, like fireworks, exploding across a horizontal canvas and the way it lit up the stratosphere. The colorful glowing of the clouds that resembled the nebulas she had painted, but in a more spectacular pageantry that danced across the top of the planet. It was a display of colors and lights that dazzled her senses. Nevaeh couldn't help but marvel at it.

If what she was going to see when she entered Gerald's world was anything as wonderful as this, she knew she'd be in for a treat. The one thing though, that she knew for certain, was this world was big! The closer she flew towards it, the more details she saw. She saw the pointed white caps of mountain ranges that so often poked the clouds in the sky.

She witnessed so many shades of blue circling around the land masses. She saw beige lands, green lands, bright white lands, and at night she saw lights, so many lights. They speckled across those lands, long lines that merged and accumulated largely in specific circular areas, and some lights that dotted areas so far away that they seemed lost.

Nevaeh just sat there hovering above the planet, watching it spin for days. She watched those lights move, grow, dim. She watched fires start and fade. She watched as small lights soared up into the sky, traveled long distances across the clouds, and then land elsewhere on the planet.

Each night Nevaeh returned to the planet. Each night she flew closer, just a little bit closer. It was so beautiful to see from this distance. But more impressive – the closer she flew, the more she heard!

She heard noise at first, a lot of noise. A barrage of machines, talking, and thunder. But each night, she focused on one sound. Thunder took her from lightning to cities full of people, sitting in their houses awaiting the storms to end. Those cities took her to people and talking. That talking took her to mass conversations, people expressing thoughts, desires...

Then she heard voices turn into song, music, the most delightful music. So many types of melodies, from vocals to instrumentals – she was amazed at how many sounds they could make. There were slow songs and fast songs, songs with a twang, and songs with a beat. There were loud, electric songs and soft, acoustic songs. Drums of all sorts, loud, leather, metal... she was entranced just listening to it all.

When Nevaeh finally decided she wanted to venture into the world her heart fluttered. What was she going to see first? The oceans? The mountains? The prairies? Which animals would she meet first? Where would she find soft, fluffy, white bunnies?

"How is Nevaeh doing?" Gerald asked one day of his son, Benjamin.

"She's good. She's been telling us all about her adventures; the sights, and sounds."

"Has she met the people yet?"

"Oddly enough, she's been taking it slowly." Benjamin admitted with relief. "I fully expected her to zoom right in there, but she hasn't yet."

"I had hoped she'd take it all in." Gerald admitted. "I told her the story about how you were born into the Painting. The reason I did it that way was so that you could grow up in the world, learning it; that there is so much to experience and know, so many joys and so many dangers."

"Dangers. What did you tell her about the dangers?" Benjamin's breathing quickened.

"You know she will be safe, right? No one can hurt her. No one can touch her. No buildings can fall on her."

"I know you've told me this, but she's my little girl, how can I not worry?"

"Of course you will worry – as I did, when my only son was born into that world. But the difference was that you were there in the flesh.

Your skin could bleed, your eyes could burn. Every pain you felt, I too felt. But you did so much good! You must remember that."

Benjamin nodded and lowered his head, "Just tell me she will be okay."

"She will be better than okay."

The day Nevaeh touched down on the ground was still many weeks after she had decided to do so. The closer she got to the ground, the more she saw. She explored hills and valleys, flew through dark caves, seeing crystallized formations. She discovered a vast underground world of caves that took her to depths even her own father had never seen.

Last week, at one point, Benjamin suggested she explore the oceans before she touched down on ground. He told her all about his love of the water. How he used to fish and swim on hot days to cool off. Then he told her about how his human body held limitations, like how he couldn't stay under the water because he couldn't hold his breath that long.

"You don't have to hold your breath. You can swim down into the depths of the oceans and see sea life and creatures no one has ever seen – except for my father who painted them."

So she did.

She described these creatures to him, seafaring dragons, eight legged ghostly octopods, fish with glowing heads and tentacles, an array of creepy crawlies, and so much more.

She explored the multitudes of colorful corals, followed underwater rivers to worlds much like the one she hovered above. She saw lava flowing through channels and caverns even farther below the surface of the water. And when she was ready to go to land, Benjamin described to her the wonders of the forests.

He knew he was prolonging the inevitable, but he also knew that as soon as she met the humans, as soon as their lives started playing out before her – she'd lose sight of the wonders of the planet. So he told her about the trees, how tall they were, how their limbs provided housing for so many animals. He told her about the day he described the tree to his friends. He gave her the speech he had given, and she hung on to every word.

So she explored the forests. She walked the pathways through the canopy of leaves. She heard trickling streams, as water flowed over smooth pebbles. She heard bird songs, insects chirping, and she watched spiders build intricate webs that sparkled in the morning dew.

She witnessed the complexities of the natural world, watching the birth of plants and animals, flowers blooming for the first time, moss spreading across stones, and mushrooms peeking through fallen leaves.

She learned about reptiles, water and land venturing creatures, and frogs that were born as tadpoles but grew to hop on land. Turtles with their thick hard shells, snakes that slithered and snails that moved incredibly slow were special learning experiences.

She met birds of all colors, shapes and sizes. Each type of bird had their own song, their own unique features. Some cawed while others chirped. Some whistled while others hooted. Some were so massive they could have almost been scary, especially when she saw others that were so small and fast, their wings fluttered faster than her eyes could see.

She met monkeys, of all shapes and sizes. She watched them use their hands to solve intricate puzzles, like how to break into coconuts to retrieve food. Some of the creatures blended so well into their environment that she could have missed them, except for their ooh-ooh-ah-ah calls. There were flying squirrels and other tree-going creatures; some were quick, some were slow. But each and every creature she laid her eyes on was unique in its own way.

She spent weeks exploring forests and jungles all over the planet. She witnessed how different each tree was, from the large leaves to the small. She saw trees that were so tall they could have touched the sky and she witnessed saplings just emerging from their seeds within the dirt, only to begin their struggle of growing.

And then she saw a beauty like no other. She observed the sun's rays streaking through the open patches of leaves, illuminating pathways. The golden white light was mystifying as it speckled the ground with shadows. And as she looked up at it, she was drawn towards it. She emerged from the edge of the forest and was struck by the brightness of the day light.

When her eyes set on the scene ahead of her, the road that led into a town, she realized, it was now time to meet the people.

Chapter 7

When Nevaeh stepped into the town she was taken aback by the hustle and bustle. Everyone was busy. And everyone was unique.

Each person looked different. They had distinctive hair colors, altering lengths, designs and shapes. Their body structure and contours varied, some were tall, some short while others round or thin. Each person wore something specific to their own style, a diverse mix of clothes in an array of styles, colors, shapes.

There were short shoes and tall shoes, and all of those shoes were moving!

Some of the people were carrying bags of goods, others were walking across the street, entering stores. Some were working, sweeping, washing windows, while others fed livestock. There was a person handing out papers, one was running and sweating, while yet another was sitting on the sidewalk holding out a cup watching people go by. It was overwhelming to Nevaeh to see so much motion at once.

She sat on a nearby bench just watching the people. It was easier to watch them when she was sitting still, but all she witnessed was short blurbs of everybody's life. She was only able to see the people as they walked from one section of town to the next. When they turned a corner, went into a building, or moved far enough away, she'd lose sight of them. She began to wonder if she should pick someone and follow them, but then she began wondering who? How could she pick just one person when everyone was so fascinating?

As she sat there pondering, a sound caught her attention. It was a small high pitched cry that seemed scared and sad. She followed the sound to a drainage culvert and looked in. There she saw a tiny kitten stuck at the bottom. It couldn't climb out and there was no way for it to squeeze through the bars and venture further into the drain. It was trapped.

Without thinking, Nevaeh reached in to pick up the kitten, but she watched her hands flow right through it. She tried a couple of times before she realized that she couldn't touch the poor animal. She stood, turned to the first person walking by her and spoke, "Can you help the kitten?"

The person didn't acknowledge her, they just kept walking. She tried the next person, "Excuse me, Sir..." He kept moving. "Ma'am, would you mind..." The woman kept going.

Nevaeh tried over and over again to attract someone's attention to no avail. She looked back down at the kitten. It was dirty, hungry, thirsty and tired. Nevaeh knew that kitten needed help, and soon, or it would die. Just then, she saw a young girl, about the same age as she, walking up. She was dragging her feet, looking in the windows, slowing down her mother's stride.

Suddenly, Nevaeh had a good feeling about this little girl. She ran to her and spoke as they walked down the sidewalk. "There's a kitten up ahead in a drainage culvert. It's hungry and thirsty. I think that kitten has been trapped there for a long time. I need you to help that kitten. Would you please help that kitten?"

The girl didn't respond. She didn't even look towards Nevaeh. Knowing she had to try again, Nevaeh gathered all of her hope for this kitten and barked, "You have to help the kitten!"

The girl stopped and looked around. A moment later, her mother pulled her back towards her to get her walking again.

That kind of worked, Nevaeh thought to herself, I need to believe it more, I have to desire it... like Grampa said. The girl was quickly getting away from her, and they were just a few feet away from the culvert. Another few steps and they'd walk past the kitten. Panic filled Nevaeh's heart. It was now or never.

Pulling every hope and desire she had for saving the kitten, letting it fill her heart, she ran. She ran towards the girl so fast, with no other thought than the kitten and before she could even think, she accidentally ran through the girl. As Nevaeh skid to a stop to turn to the girl and face her, she noticed the girl had come to an abrupt stop. She looked around, as if someone had tapped her shoulder and disappeared. Her mother pulled at her arm, but she refused to move. She kept looking around, and then, she looked down.

"Momma, look!"

"What is it?" The mother demanded. The little girl kneeled down by the culvert to get a better look.

"What are you doing down there?" the mother inquired with annoyance.

"Momma, there's a kitten in there!"

The mother leaned over and looked. Suddenly the kitten, the frail, skinny kitten who barely had any energy left at all –meowed the most pitiful yowl.

"Oh, the poor little baby!" she cried. She kneeled down and reached into the culvert, but her arms were too short. Realizing she needed help, she looked up at a tall man walking by. "Sir, would you please help me?"

He looked at the woman and girl on their knees and peered into the drain. Spotting the kitten, he inquired, "Is that yours?"

"No, but it needs help. I can't reach it."

He looked at it again and then at the arms of his suit. He had no intention of getting his suit jacket dirty. He stood there, mulling over the problem for a moment, when another man walked up to them.

"What's going on?"

The woman and child explained the situation. This man seemed more amicable towards helping so the other man in the suit just walked away. Nevaeh watched him leave for a moment and shook her head with disappointment. She couldn't understand how anyone would see this predicament and NOT help. The thought was really bothering her when the scene grabbed her attention and redirected her back to the kitten.

The second man kneeled down next to the two ladies. He reached in and grabbed the kitten, scooping up the tiny fur ball in his large, warm hands. When he pulled the kitten out, into the daylight, the little girl reached for it. The man relinquished the cat to the young girl who thanked him.

Cradling the kitten in her arms she noticed how skinny it was. "Momma, it's gotta be hungry. You can see his ribcage."

Just then a little boy and his father walked up. "What's that?" The little boy asked.

"It's a kitten we just rescued."

The little boy reached to pet the kitten, then looked up at his dad. "Hey Pop, we were just heading to the pet store to get a kitten, why not just take this one home?"

"Son, look how scrawny and dirty it is. It probably won't make it."

"But Dad, we'll never know if we don't try. Please?" The little boy pleaded.

When the father finally let in, the little girl relinquished the kitten into the boy's arms and looked back up at her mom. "We did a really good thing just now, didn't we?"

"We surly did, Sweetheart. We surly did!"

Chapter 8

When Nevaeh woke the next morning she leapt from her bed, raced downstairs and ran up to her father. "Daddy, Daddy, I have to talk to Grampa right now!"

"It's a bit early to call him," Benjamin glanced at the time. "Can you wait?"

"No."

A few minutes later Nevaeh was reporting her uplifting tale about saving the kitten to her grandfather over the phone. She described how she talked one child into saving it and how the kitten even found a home. Her grandfather, as well as her father (who was listening in) was quite pleased.

"That is a wonderful story." he exclaimed happily. "I am so glad you shared it with me."

"But Grampa, I have questions."

"Okay, what are your questions?"

"Why can no one see me? Why do my hands go through things? Why didn't the adults hear me? Why did the other girl only hear me when I went through her? Why did the tall guy in the suit not help? And why…"

"Whoa, Sweetie, one question at a time," Gerald stopped her. "The first two questions we discussed before. You are only there in spirit. You will only be able to see and hear. You won't be able to talk with or touch the people."

Gerald then added, "Why didn't the adults hear you? It could have been a multitude of reasons. Maybe they don't normally listen to children. Maybe they were too busy or preoccupied to hear you..."

"The little girl looked like she may have heard me, but it wasn't until I accidently ran through her that she looked down and saw the kitten. Why?"

Gerald smiled. "Think about the wind. You can't see it. You can't touch it, but you can feel it. You can sense that it is there because whatever it does: going through the leaves of trees, moving wind chimes or swooshing around a big building, it makes itself known. The wind itself isn't visible, the wind by itself doesn't make a noise - but its presence does."

"So I am like the wind. I can be felt if I..."

"Make waves." Benjamin added.

"All you have to do is be a strong enough presence to be felt, and you'll be able to do some miraculous feats!"

Later that day Benjamin looked outside the window to see Nevaeh sitting in the field looking up into the sky. Every time the wind blew she'd raise her arms to feel it move around her. He was entranced watching her study it. He was curious as to what deep thoughts were going through his little girl's head, but he let her be. She needed this time to study.

That evening she excused herself to go to bed early. "Are you sure? We were going to play a family game."

"Please, Daddy? I want to go practice what I learned today in the Painting."

"Alright." Benjamin conceded. He smiled as he watched her race upstairs.

The next morning Nevaeh was not nearly as excited as the morning before. Benjamin could see it in her face that she was not at all happy. "What's wrong, Sweetheart?"

"It didn't work!"

"What didn't work?"

"Nothing! Nothing worked! And I just don't understand it at all!"

"Start from the beginning and tell me everything." Benjamin sat down at the table and readied himself for a long tale.

Nevaeh told him how she flew into the town and began trying to knock people's hats from their heads, like the wind does, how she tried to slam doors closed like the wind. She tried to jostle unsuspecting horses. She tried to stop a ball in mid-air, and how she tried to pick a flower. "I just don't understand why none of it worked!"

Benjamin sat there stunned. He couldn't believe his sweet, innocent daughter could try all of those troublesome things. He sat there for a moment trying to pull from his father's many teachings, how best to approach this situation.

"Do you remember what Grampa Gerald told you about his Painting? About how he designed it?" Nevaeh shrugged her shoulders. "Do you remember us telling you about good deeds? About how he coated the world with aspirations of goodness..."

Nevaeh interrupted, "I remember when you said 'One small act can mean so much'."

"Exactly." He scowled at her lovingly. "Your grandfather painted that world so anyone who had the will, the desire to do *Good*, will have a way to do it. He gave everybody the chance to be the solution, to answer his call and help others by just listening and feeling. Everything within the Painting, everything he intended for it to be, is all about doing good deeds. Making the world a better place."

Nevaeh smiled as she remembered.

"Now, do you know why everything you tried to do last night, didn't work?"

Nevaeh thought about it for a bit and then spoke. "I wasn't trying to do good things."

"That's right. The things you were trying to do either wasn't nice or was self-serving. You weren't trying to do good for others. You didn't have the desire to help people, you just wanted to play. That is not the reason you were given the gift to enter the Painting, was it?"

"No Sir."

"I think you should excuse yourself and think about this conversation. You get to go to this amazing world and watch the most phenomenal things take place and you – if you want it bad enough – can make this place, this wondrous world so much better, simply by wanting it. You've been given a gift, an extraordinary gift, and all you have to do is make sure that everything you do is always with the purest intentions.

"Yes, Daddy."

As Nevaeh sulked away slowly, Benjamin smiled as he recalled all of the important life lessons his father shared with him growing up. He remembered feeling confused like Nevaeh felt just now, and being overwhelmed with the knowledge he was gaining. He remembered growing up inside the Painting. He was trying so hard to live his life with the purest intentions, when the playfulness of just being a child would overwhelm his senses.

He also remembered the day that his best friends talked about feeling sorry for him for not being able to just be a child, for knowing so much and having so much weight on his small shoulders. It made him sad for just a moment, knowing that his friends worried about him, but then it encouraged him because he was more grown up than even the grown-ups sometimes.

Knowledge is power. The more he learned, the more he taught, the better he felt. The easier it became for him to face any challenges life threw at him.

Benjamin suddenly had an overwhelming urge to call his father.

Chapter 9

The next night when Nevaeh flew back into the Painting she flew to the town she had grown so accustomed to and walked around.

She actually found being here kind of boring. The people were always so busy doing their daily tasks. Working, cleaning, cooking, sleeping, they hardly ever played or relaxed. Plus, there was so many of them. To her it was like watching the chaos of a disturbed ant bed. Everyone had their own individual tasks but if you didn't know what each task was you'd lose them in the shuffle.

As she walked around, trying to keep up with one person, someone more interesting would grab her attention. She'd turn to follow that person until someone else caught her attention. She was crisscrossing all over the town having only glimpsed a fraction of its people and she was growing exhausted. She hadn't learned anything about the people, except that they never stopped to appreciate their beautiful world.

As she sat down on a nearby bench she looked around at the nature around her. It was beautiful and colorful. The animals knew how to appreciate the world. The birds would sing, the turtles would sun bathe, the flowers would bloom brightly showing such joy to simply be alive. Why couldn't the people do the same?

Maybe that was how she could help, Nevaeh thought. Maybe it was her task to help the people learn how to enjoy themselves, and to appreciate the simple things in life. She walked up to a mother who was busy trying to keep her children in tow. She had a baby on one hip, a toddler holding her hand, and an older sibling trudging along slowly behind her, causing her to constantly turn and harp on him to "keep up." This reminded her about her own mother, and suddenly a plan came to her.

She approached the first person nearest the mother and spoke, "Give her a flower." The person kept walking, but Nevaeh was not deterred. She walked with the woman and kept speaking out loud enough for anyone nearby to hear her, "Someone, please give this woman a flower! Look how hard she is working. Look how tired she is. I know that when I give my mommy a flower, it makes her pause and smile. So would someone please, give this nice woman a flower?"

Just then a man bent down to tie his shoe. While crouched down a bird dropped a daisy on the ground in front of him. Curiously he picked it up and returned to a standing position. He looked around and saw the mother coming up the sidewalk. Something inside him made him want to give her this flower, so as she neared he approached her.

"I want to give this to you."

She stopped and looked at the man, then at the flower in his hand. A tear started to form in her eyes as she looked up into the man's face and asked, "Why?"

"I remember how hard my own mother worked to raise my brothers and me. I just felt the desire to give this to you."

"Mom?" The toddler looked up at the flower curiously. "Is that for Jenny?"

The mother burst out crying.

"I'm so sorry ma'am." The man backed away slightly. "I didn't mean to upset you."

"Oh, no, I'm sorry, sir! I should explain."

"You don't have to."

"Please let me." She placed her hand on the man's hand. "Jenny was my oldest daughter, she loved daisies. She would draw them all of the time."

"Might I inquire as to why it seems you are talking about her in the past tense?"

"She passed away one year ago today. I've been going all over town looking for a daisy to take to her grave site but they are out of season. I was just about to give up."

He placed the daisy in her hand. "Then this daisy is for your daughter, Jenny."

"But sir, how did you know?"

"I didn't. I just had a feeling that you needed it. I guess the only thing I could say, is thanks to Geody."

"Thanks to Geody!"

The next day Gerald stopped by to check on Nevaeh. She was sitting at the table eating breakfast when she saw him walk in. With a full

mouth and holding her spoon in the air, she burst out with a question that had been bugging her all morning. "Grampa who is Geody?"

"Are they still using that name?" Gerald smiled as he pulled out a chair and sat down next to her at the table. "How funny."

"Are *you* Geody?"

"I guess I am." He smiled. "You see, my father, your great grandfather was insistent that after I finished painting the world that I sign my creation. He once told me that signing your art is an important part of the creative process. The instant you apply your name to your work, you declare it officially finished and ready to be seen by the world. No matter what your signature looks like, what form it takes or where you put it, no work of art will ever be complete without one. Your signature identifies your art for all time as having been created, completed and approved of by you and you alone. You are the creator for now and all time."

"Wow," Nevaeh cooed but interrupted her grandfather's deep thoughts. "But why do they call you Geody?"

"Because that was what they saw." He laughed out loud. He reached for a pen and paper and started to draw. "My first thought, because my name is so long, Gerald Oliver Delaney, was that I would just put my initials." He drew his G.

"But then I realized that the G took up every bit of space that I had in that small unoccupied part of the ocean. If I wanted to add my O and D I'd need to make them smaller, maybe even place them artistically inside my G. So I did." Gerald drew his initials just like he had painted them on the Painting so many years before.

"Over the years, people stopped referring to my initials as G. O. D. and instead lost the pauses and spelled out the letters. That's how I started getting called Geody."

"That's funny." Nevaeh smiled as she looked at her grandfather's drawing. "You know, it kind of looks like a face."

Gerald glanced at it and smiled. "I can see that." He looked at Nevaeh who was deep in thought.

"Maybe that's why everyone says that you are always watching over them. Because you drew your face right into the Painting."

Chapter 10

After her meal, Nevaeh returned her thoughts back to the Painting and last night's activities. She told her grandfather how the daisy made the mother so happy that she cried and the reason why she cried. "Grampa, how did the man get the daisy?"

"Well, you said a bird dropped it."

"Yeah, but how did the bird know?"

"I painted them to know. The animals are more in tune to the happenings of the world than the humans could ever grasp. They know when something is coming, like a storm or earthquake. They know when someone is feeling sad or angry. They know how to care for the people, if they're allowed to, and they know what needs to happen when the desire is there."

"But how could the bird know that the flower I asked for needed to be a daisy. I didn't know it should have been a daisy, so how could the bird know?"

"How did you know the mother needed a flower in the first place?"

"I didn't. I just thought it would make her happy, like my mommy."

"So you knew she was sad?"

"No..." Nevaeh thought, "I don't think so."

"But something in you made you want to give that specific woman a flower, right?"

"Right."

"That is how my Painting works." Gerald smiled. "Everything is connected. Every little thing, every big thing, every plant, animal and human. You simply helped to reinforce what needed to happen with your desire to get the task done for her."

"So when I wanted to give the woman a flower, the Painting knew exactly which flower and told the bird to find a daisy and give it to the man to give to the woman."

"That's right."

"But wait," Nevaeh realized, "Why didn't the bird just drop the flower by the mother?"

"You said she had a baby on her hip, a toddler in her hand and that she kept looking back at the older child, right?"

"Yes."

"Do you think with all that she had going on, that she would look down as she walked and see a daisy laying on the ground?"

"Probably not." Nevaeh agreed, but then she thought of something else. "The bird could have landed on her to give her the flower."

"True." Gerald agreed, but then added his own question for Nevaeh. "But, wouldn't that have startled her?"

"Maybe."

"And if she would have been startled, she might have dropped the child."

"I didn't think of that."

"Besides," Gerald added, "no one else would have known why that daisy was so important, not even you. The man that helped wouldn't have become an instrument of good. He wouldn't have heard her story or learned how easy it was to do something nice for somebody else. He wouldn't have walked away feeling good about himself, or to tell anyone else how great it made him feel."

Gerald observed Nevaeh's smile stretch across her face, then heard something he decided to add to his story. "Additionally, a few days have passed on the Painting as of now. I just heard the man bump into that mother on the street again. They struck up a conversation and he's going to see her again tonight."

"He is?"

"It seems the father of those children passed away as well."

"He did?" Sadness flushed across Nevaeh's face.

"But I have a good feeling that your single act of kindness, is going to become a future for those people."

"Really?" Nevaeh's eyes brightened. "How?"

"I can see things flowing. He's going to check in on that lady and her family, and to be available for them if they need him. Eventually, they all will become closer. Friendship will turn to more and at some point, if all goes well, who knows? Maybe those children will get another father figure in their lives."

"Wow." Nevaeh took that in thoughtfully. "It's like a ripple," she concluded.

"What's like a ripple?" Benjamin spoke as he walked into the room. Seeing his father and daughter sitting at the table, he pulled out a chair and sat with them.

"The good deed I did. It's like an ever expanding ripple in the water. It keeps spreading outward, until it changes the course of the lives it touches."

Benjamin smiled knowingly. "A simple act of caring creates an endless ripple."

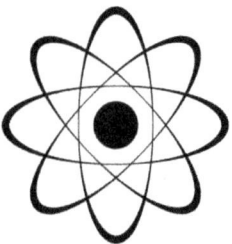

Chapter 11

When Nevaeh returned to the Painting she made a point to check in on the mother and her children. She watched how the man would check in on them from time to time. Over the course of many visits, or in the timeline of the Painting, many years, Nevaeh watched that couple grow closer, get married and flourish.

Every once in a while they'd thank Geody for bringing them together. They'd tell friends about the day they met. How Geody made it happen. How it was like his spirit pushed him to offer this woman a flower and how miraculous it was that a daisy just happened to land in front of him. Nevaeh found the entire story to be quite inspiring. Especially because she saw herself as the spirit that helped it happen.

In the meantime, Nevaeh had done quite a few good deeds throughout the Painting. She had encouraged unsuspecting people to feed the hungry, water the thirsty, and help the elderly.

One day not so long ago, Nevaeh was sitting on the bench watching the hustle and bustle of the people. She saw what she would learn to be a blind man slowly making his way down the sidewalk. He used a stick to find obstacles before he tripped. He used it to approximate distance like when the curb dropped down.

People avoided him as he walked, so they wouldn't get in his way, or accidentally trip him, which Nevaeh found good, but when the bag he was carrying developed a hole and an apple fell out, Nevaeh jumped into action.

The blind man had stopped walking. He was using his stick to sweep the walkway searching for his lost apple, but accidentally tapping people's feet as they walked by. Some of the pedestrians grimaced or groaned as they attempted to avoid the man. Another bumped into him and feigned a fake apology as he kept walking by. The jostling though, shifted another apple from the blind man's bag.

Nevaeh heard the man let out a rather dismayed, "ohhh..." and she could hear in his voice that he was flustered as to what to do.

"Hey, did you see that?" Nevaeh addressed the crowd. "He's losing items from his bag. He can't see where they fell, but you can! Someone please help him." Nevaeh stood between the man who couldn't see and the apple that fell from his bag and she willed the bystanders to do something. As another apple rolled through the hole in his bag, she pressed harder for someone to help. "There goes another apple. Would someone please help this man? He can't see where they are."

Just then a woman noticed the apple on the ground, and another apple ahead of her. She looked around to see whom it may have belonged to and saw the blind man looking overwhelmed and confused. She hastily picked up both apples and rushed up to the man. She called to him just as another apple slipped through the hole.

"Sir, your apples are dropping from a hole in your bag." He reached for the hole in his bag when she placed the two apples in his free hand. He fumbled to hold them as she retrieved the third apple on the ground. As she attempted to hand him the third apple, he clasped both of his hands together and dropped his walking stick.

A fellow bystander picked up his stick and realized the dilemma. He pulled his sandwich from the bag he was carrying it in and offered the bag to the lady. "It's not very big, but will this help?"

"Yes, it will." She smiled as she dropped an apple in it and then took it from his hand. She took the other two apples from the blind man's hands and placed them in, as the bystander returned the walking stick.

"You two are very kind to help me." The man spoke softly. "May Geody bless you."

Once the two of them had resolved the issue of the falling apples, the blind man thanked the both of them and started on his way. The two looked at each other and smiled.

"That was a very nice thing you did, to help that man." The bystander spoke with an inner delight.

"I couldn't have done it without your lunch bag." She smiled back. "He was right, that was such a kind thing to do."

"Kindness is something the deaf can hear and the blind can see."

"That's a beautiful phrase, she spoke as she looked towards the blind man almost fully across the street.

"Grampa, it was a good feeling to help that man, but why was he blind?" Nevaeh asked after talking with Gerald about the good deed she helped make happen that night.

"That is a good question, one with which I've heard many times. So let me answer your question with a question. Would the man have needed help finding his apples if he could have seen them?"

"Probably not."

"The other two people, would they have received the benefit of those feel-good emotions if he didn't need the assistance?"

"I guess not."

"And finally, is it not true that everyone in the Painting is different in a multitude of ways? Size, shape, color and affliction?"

"That's true."

"So why shouldn't this man be blind if his presence helps others and good things can come of it?"

Nevaeh thought about that for a moment and then she countered her grandfather's question. "Okay Grampa, but what about the fact that he can't see all of the beauty of your world?"

"When I take one sense, I make sure the other senses develop stronger skills. That man may not be able to see a sunset but he can hear the quietest bird chirp, the hushed rustling of leaves in a slight breeze, and he can feel more through a stick than most people notice with perfect vision. He's got abilities others can't even imagine, so why would I want to deprive him of such a unique experience?"

Each time she visited the Painting, Nevaeh continued doing good deeds. She got better at sharing her heartfelt desires with others and enacting change in small ways.

She helped people do things that they struggled with by sending passersby to help. She encouraged those with plenty to share with those who were hungry, either with extra food or their time. She opened the heart of an affluent man who helped a young girl just wanting to get an education and paid for her tuition. With every good deed and act of kindness Nevaeh was able to enact, they received a delight within. She witnessed happiness, reached a deeper understanding of life, and made the world a bit more beautiful.

Chapter 12

It had been a number of weeks, for Nevaeh, which in the Painting was about 15 years. So much had changed, the people had aged, the trees had grown taller and the buildings had been torn down and replaced with bigger, better buildings.

Nevaeh was sitting on her favorite bench, watching the hustle and bustle, wondering what she was going to do today, when a piece of paper, floating on the wind, landed on the bench beside her. She read it, to discover that a brand new veterinarian practice was opening in town, and she became curious enough to check it out.

As she watched the young man work on his advertising, handing out flyers and meeting his clients, something kept tugging at her heart. There was something familiar about this man, but she knew she had never seen him before. It wasn't until a couple brought in a kitten they found, and the man started regaling them with a story from his past, that Nevaeh realized why she was drawn to him.

"When I was a boy, my father and I were walking down the sidewalk in town when we met a young girl who needed help rescuing a trapped kitten in a storm drain. After one man rescued the cat, I got to take it home and care for it. That was the most magical day for me, because that was the day I decided to dedicate my life towards helping animals.

You see, nursing the kitten back to health, bottle feeding it, helping it to walk, to grow, was more rewarding than I would have ever imagined. Learning how easy it was to save a life opened my eyes to possibilities I had never dreamed of. I started rescuing all sorts of critters as I grew up. I nursed multiple baby squirrels who fell from their nests. I mended bird's broken wings, helped turtles heal broken shells, and I can't even begin to tell you how many cats and dogs I helped nurse back to health from bite wounds, broken legs, chipped teeth and more.

For me, that one simple act opened doors I didn't even know existed. I realized I would grow up to become a veterinarian and I've been sharing my story to help others realize their potential ever since."

"That's a wonderful story." The client spoke as the Vet peered into the kitten's mouth.

Just then a woman walked in, "Sorry to bother you, but your ten o clock just arrived."

"Thank you. I'll be right out."

After she closed the door, the client watched the vet check the kitten's ears and temperature and then spoke again. "I wonder what happened to the young girl who originally discovered the trapped kitten?"

"Funny you'd ask..." he smiled as he looked up at the client. "That was she just now."

"Really?"

"That little girl came by to check on the kitten often after I took it home. We became friends. She helped me with many of my critter-saving ventures and eventually, we got married."

The client smiled brightly. "Wow, Geody sure does work in mysterious ways."

"That he does."

Nevaeh learned that it was her desire, her push for someone to help that kitten that day, that made the action take place. But now, she beamed brightly, realizing that her one simple act of kindness had trickled down the line and had done so much good. That her will to help that one kitten had also willed these two souls together, to become friends and then chose to go into the field of helping other unfortunate animals... the knowledge was overwhelming and beautiful.

When she awoke that morning she called her Grampa Gerald to tell him about it. She just couldn't keep the thrill inside and not share it with others.

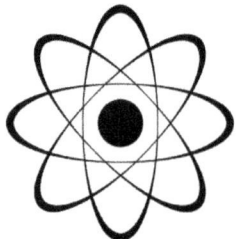

Chapter 13

Over time, Nevaeh explored many towns and cities. She ventured into small country communities and large bustling metropolises. She found the big cities to be overwhelming, but beautiful. She was inspired how the people could build such intricate communities and thrive living so close to one another. But she also found it noisy.

The people, the traffic, the vehicles and workers – everything was so close together, all of the noises blended together. And yet, it was those people who enjoyed the noises. They would talk about it as if it were a song, an orchestra of sounds all working together to make a wondrous place.

Crying babies, car horns honking, and jack hammers breaking up concrete completely drowned out any nature in the area. She couldn't hear the birds, she couldn't focus on the plants and she missed the flowers. Sure there were stores that sold flowers, all sorts of beautiful flowers brought in from all over the world. But they had been cut and kept cold to preserve their beauty, and because they had been refrigerated, they had lost what smell they used to have.

Granted Nevaeh couldn't smell them, but she could see the people as they'd walk by and stop to smell the flowers and simply shrug their shoulders and move on. It was completely different than what she had seen before in smaller communities. There flowers grew along the sides of the road and apparently smelled so good, they'd breathe deeply of the aromas and bask in the scent over a long few moments. The flowers also attracted bees and butterflies and hummingbirds.

She realized she would never get bored here in the big city, where there was something going on everywhere. There was dancing in the street, artwork on the building walls, music from the subways, singing from the upper windows of nearby buildings. People all over were finding ways to share their creativity with the world, and yet, so few people truly noticed them. However, the people who did notice the talents that were being shared, well, they were truly the blessed ones.

Nevaeh would then travel to smaller communities, towns that were so small there was only a couple of small stores. There people would travel more than an hour to get their needs met in nearby cities, because they thrived in the small country living their lives offered.

They were so close to nature, and to the animals. They rode horses, milked cows and spent long Saturdays fishing. It was so quiet you could hear the crickets chirping, the wind whistling, and the neighbors hunting. They held rodeos to show off their talents and skills, and they had dances and social gatherings to get together and catch up with each other's lives.

They walked slower, talked slower, and took their time because all they had was time. And yet, when their children were old enough to decide what they wanted to do with their lives, Nevaeh witnessed many times how some chose to stay while others chose to go. They had a desire to do something grand, to be a part of something bigger, to venture into the big city and make something of themselves. It was almost baffling to her, but she watched it nevertheless.

Maybe it was because Nevaeh could choose where she wanted to go, maybe because she had seen so many different places in this world that she had figured out the best locations, or maybe it was because she had figured out what her own desires were, that Nevaeh decided to venture back to the town she had started from.

She asked her father about it one day, after bouncing from town to town and city to city over the course of many years. His response was fairly simplistic.

"Maybe you went back to that town because it's familiar, and because you have so many connections there already."

While she had accepted that as a good excuse, she kind of knew in the back of her mind that it wasn't entirely true.

Over the course of the many years she spent traveling the world, visiting all of the various countries on each continent, getting to know the cultures and people, she knew one thing to be true – the people she had first met in that little town, were either quite old or had long ago passed away.

The town had changed, and it had grown. It wasn't as big as a city, but it was busier than it ever was before. So many new buildings and houses and schools and roads had been constructed. The landscape she remembered had changed drastically. Suburbs touched the city and sprawled down the road towards other small towns; communities were annexed in.

From outer space their once speckled lights at night that dotted the terrain, became just as bright and overflowing as some of the other big cities. Her park bench where she had spent so many afternoons just sitting and watching the people had been removed, along with the park, for a shopping mall.

Nevaeh may have returned to the town she had first met, but the town had not returned to her. She journeyed to the edges of the metropolis, to smaller, outer communities and found moderate, isolated subdivisions that were scattered around landscapes of forests and glens. Floating above the communities, she could see how they kept spreading outwards. She watched them cutting down trees to pave new roads and foundations.

She did what she could for the people, but the growth was engulfing. It consumed everything in its place to make room for future generations. She was witnessing how the small cities became the big cities and how so many people would pack themselves into this crowded area. She watched them lose sight of what was important in life because there was so much to do to keep them busy.

But then she caught sight of those who decided to move farther out, so they could be back in the simpler lives they so longed for. She followed them into smaller communities that seemed so familiar, but each day the city encroached on the outskirts. Growth was happening so quickly, it felt as if Nevaeh couldn't keep up.

Every time Neveah returned to the Painting, so much time had passed, she felt as if she was a stranger looking in.

When she finally went to her father about how she was feeling it reminded him of a story he had once heard.

"When I was living in the Painting I remember spending a good amount of time in one town that needed the extra help. They had built a dam to create a lake. It was a beautiful lake and brought a lot of happiness, but one overly wet spring that town got a lot of rain. They didn't think to let the water out of the lake until it was too late. When the water went over the top of the spillway, an area designed to keep the water from going over the top of the dam, it flowed across the land, sweeping trees and plants downstream. It cut into the land and carved out a deep gorge. It caused a lot of damage downstream."

"That's horrible Daddy, but what's the point of your story?"

"In so many ways, life in the Painting is like water. It keeps rushing forward with such power that it can be destructive. There are times in life when the people can feel like they're drowning. Times when they have so much to do, so many tasks that are being asked of them, that it makes their course seem already cut out and out of control.

But there is also something else to take into account with water. Water, that can be so overpowering, so destructive, brings life. We need water to survive. We don't have the power to control it, but we can calm it. We can direct its path with planning and foresight. We can guide it and change the course it takes, and they could have done that, too.

With one simple act of caring, you can create an endless ripple."

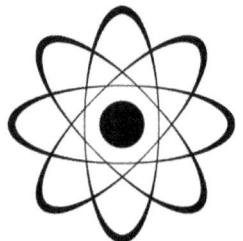

Chapter 14

That evening Nevaeh returned to the Painting and soared over the lands looking for something specific, a gorge. When she found one, not knowing if it was the right one or not, she stopped to investigate. She scoured the land dotted by rivers and hills, large and small patches of trees, clusters of boats on the water and trails leading up from the lake into the forested areas.

That's when she spotted the lookout. A beautiful area at the top of a hill overlooking the gorge and the lake. It was a panorama of what should have been a postcard, a breath-taking sight to marvel at, and at the moment, the sun was setting and glistening upon the exposed stone of the gorge.

She was gazing out at the beauty when she heard the shuffle of someone's feet approaching. She turned and looked at the elderly man and watched him advance towards the guardrail at the edge of the cliff. He beheld the sight and breathed in the artistry of the landscape. He then pulled a picture out of his wallet and looked at it.

"Martha, do you remember that day? The day we watched the water just starting to trickle onto the spillway? I remember thinking how slow it was rising, that everyone on the news was over-reacting. But then the stories began to flow like the river that water was becoming. Before long the flood waters were ten foot tall and pouring over the landscape like a jack-hammer. They swept away trees, ground, rocks and boulders. The waters scrubbed the land clear of everything and then kept flowing. It connected to the nearby river and rushed downstream so fast. It overflowed the river beds, saturated everything downstream, picked up homes, and we watched those homes float down the rushing waters like an out of control canoe... that's how I feel right now... without you." He looked up from the picture clasped within his palm at the sight.

Nevaeh witnessed a tear slip from his eye. She wondered if Martha was his wife... she wondered if Martha was gone.

At that moment, the elderly man clutched his chest, and groaned in pain. His left hand grasped the railing as his knees began to buckle. Nevaeh realized he was in pain, and something dire was happening to his body. She looked around and saw no one. This man needed help and she couldn't do anything for him – she looked around, desperate to find help when she saw a deer.

He was staring at Nevaeh, his head and neck straight up, his eyes wide. Maybe he was concerned about the old man, who had just fallen to his knees, the strain apparent on his wrinkled face. Nevaeh looked back at the deer, who seemed to look right at her, and then he turned and ran into the woods.

"Wait!" She called as she flew after him. She flew into the woods and followed the path he was on. He leaped over the makeshift steps built from logs and tree roots. He ascended up a hill and then he disappeared over the top. When Nevaeh sailed over the top of the hill she flew right through a couple taking a walk on the nature trail. As she flew through them, her thoughts and worry for the elderly man went through them. She skid to a stop and turned to face the two.

"Did you hear that?" One said to the other.

"What?"

"That rustling, it sounded like a deer or something large running down the trail."

"Nope." He answered back. He turned to continue along the trail when he was stopped again.

"Are you sure that's the way? There's a fork in the trail here."

"Yeah, we go left." He pointed to the trail he was intending to walk down.

"But I thought we were going to see the gorge. Wouldn't that be up and to the right?" She inquired as she pointed the same direction she had heard the rustling.

"You just want to see if you can spot the deer." He chuckled.

"Well neither of us have been out here before, how can you be so sure that is the correct way?"

"I can't." They both looked at the trails ahead of them attempting to make a decision.

Nevaeh was screaming at them, "Go right! Go right!" She was desperate for them to go that way so they could check on the elderly man. So when she saw the man take a step towards the trail to the left, she panicked. She flew down the trail, turned and was about to fly through him again when her presence spooked a mother bird. She flew from her nest and towards the man stepping towards her and dive-bombed him. He ducked, covering his head and called to his wife, "Go right – run!"

The bird squawked and chased them up the path until they were far enough away from her nest to feel safe again. They continued to sprint up the path until they felt it was 'safe again' and then slowed to a stop.

Laughing at each other and the adrenaline escaping their system, they bent over to catch their breath. That's when the sound attracted their attention.

"Ohhh..."

They exchanged curious glances and proceeded up the path at a brisk pace. When they saw the elderly man huddled on the ground, they jumped into action.

Nevaeh was relieved when they found the man, helped him, called for help, and found assistance to help him off the mountain and to the hospital. She realized it had been a joint effort. The deer led her down the path, her determination to get them to choose the right path filled the bird with the desire to lead them away from the left, and his groan of pain pulled them closer.

They had never been here before, but their arrival saved the life of an old man whose loneliness was going to take him from the world way too soon.

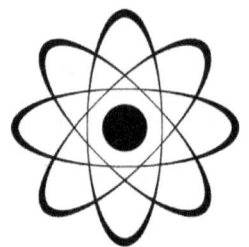

Chapter 15

"What's wrong? Gerald asked of his son when Benjamin came to him.

"It's Nevaeh, something is wrong. She's stopped visiting the Painting. She hasn't talked about it for weeks."

Gerald walked over to Nevaeh, sitting in the yard, overlooking the tadpoles in the pond, and sat down beside her. "What are you doing?"

"Watching the frogs."

Gerald looked closely at the pond and then spoke. "I don't see any frogs."

"In the water." Nevaeh pointed.

"Those are actually tadpoles. They haven't become frogs yet."

"I know that Grampa, but why lie to ourselves? They will grow up to become a frog, so why wait to change their name?"

Gerald sat down next to her and was quiet for a long time. He watched the tadpoles swim, and eat, and sleep. He saw big tadpoles with legs starting to emerge and small tadpoles fresh out of their eggs. It took him back to a day he fondly remembered from his childhood.

He recalled watching the tadpoles, like he and Nevaeh were doing right now. He was fascinated with how they could breathe under water. He remembered how enchanting he considered their world, underwater, where all you could hear was the sounds of the currents. Where your vision was enhanced because your hearing was dulled, and how nice the quiet would have been to him when he was a child.

Then Gerald remembered the kids from school - how they all decided that day to go swimming. He heard them laughing and screaming. He watched them leap into the water, splash around, kick up the mud, disrupt the ecosystem and how their presence destroyed the tadpoles home. He tried to find them through the turbulent waters, to see them through the thick muddy mess but they had all been swept away.

He remembered how sad he was, and how angry he had become. He had yelled at the children for coming – but then he realized he was upset at them for playing, for enjoying their lives and for partaking in the world of which they were a part.

They didn't understand what his problem was, but he used that to understand what was going on in Nevaeh's mind.

"It's true. They do grow up. They come out of the water. They lead their own lives and they move on. That's just the way it is. It doesn't mean that we should skip this step though."

"Grampa, it's sad to see so much change. It's hard to watch them all move on so quickly."

Gerald contemplated his next words carefully, then spoke curiously. "You know, I haven't seen that pretty blue sweater of yours in a very long time."

Nevaeh looked over at him with intrigue. "My blue sweater?"

"Yeah, the one with the sparkles."

"Grampa," she smiled, "I got rid of that months ago."

"You did?" Gerald sounded disappointed. "It looked nice on you. Why'd you get rid of it?"

"I outgrew it."

"So you just threw it away?"

"No. I donated it."

"That's sad."

"Why is it sad? I'm sure someone else is wearing it right now."

"Well I guess that's a good thing. It can go on to be enjoyed by someone else."

"Maybe that someone else's Grampa could enjoy it, too?" Nevaeh offered.

"Maybe." Gerald smiled. "It's just hard to watch you grow up so quickly. It won't be long before you move on with your life, and I get to see you even less than I do now."

"I guess you're right." Nevaeh realized. "It's what's supposed to happen, even in your Painting." She took her Grampa's hand.

"So, do you want to tell me what's really on your mind?"

"I don't feel like I fit anywhere in there."

"How do you mean?"

"Everyone is so busy. It's like they are all strangers. To me, to each other... I feel so alone when I go there now."

"I can understand that. It is heartbreaking to know how easy it is for others to move on, to feel as though your presence is either overlooked, unnoticed or completely forgotten. I have felt that way many times throughout my life." Gerald admitted sadly.

"You have?"

Gerald nodded. "In the absence of a personal connection, lack of love or a feeling of belonging, there is always suffering. But it's those hardships that strengthen you. That discomfort you are feeling is because you need to find an attachment. Something or someone that connects you to what you need."

Nevaeh looked lost. She stared at Gerald for a long moment before speaking again. "How do I do that?"

"That's an excellent question." Gerald frowned, "But only you can figure that out."

Nevaeh turned to look back at the tadpoles. This wasn't helping, she was thinking.

"Loneliness leads to heartache."

"How did you get past it?" She inquired.

"Well...." Gerald thought about it. "I returned back to the places that made me happiest... and then I made new memories, found new happiness and grew with the changes that were coming at me."

"How can I do that?"

"I know you found a lot of happiness at one time within my Painting. I think it's time to go back and make a new happiness."

"The small town I once liked is now a large metropolis. It's so loud and busy – it makes me sad to see it now."

"So find a new happiness. Find a different small town to fall in love with."

"Grampa, I traveled the world, it's all the same. So many people, so many blurry faces racing by in their busy lives, not listening, not caring, not noticing one another or the beauty of your world. Why bother?"

"Because someone there still needs you."

"How do they need me?"

"Benjamin was raised in a small town that has long been forgotten. It grew a bit, over time, but the work dried up. Many people moved and the town was almost forgotten about. But a new company has started to build there. It's brought back jobs, and people, it's about to prosper."

"That's good, I guess." Nevaeh smiled. "But doesn't that mean it'll grow into a big city and lose sight of what's important, just like all of the others?"

"Maybe. Maybe not. You see, something just happened, something that could take it all away. The town needs you to help it survive."

"But what can I do?"

"Everything. Or nothing. You don't have to do anything, but I'd like for you to at least witness what's going to happen. I think it will be quite beneficial for you."

Chapter 16

Nevaeh was told to follow the bells and as she did, she flew into a familiar looking town as the sun was setting behind the nearby hills.

The town was laid out like many towns she had visited. There was a square, where buildings of stores and restaurants were lined up along all four sides of the streets. Across the street, in the center of town, was a beautiful tree. A massively large tree, whose branches stretched out far and wide, curving towards the ground where they almost touched and then reaching towards the sky as if getting a second wind.

There were floodlights shining onto the tree from the ground and picnic benches placed methodically in even increments along the outer sidewalk. It was a beautiful place, but no one was there. It seemed a shame.

Nevaeh looked around and saw that there were a few people heading towards the school gymnasium at the end of the street. She followed the people, and as she neared, she realized the entire town may have been here. The building was packed full of people, and they were all talking among themselves.

"I can't believe we're even here talking about this. It's ludicrous to think we can save it."

"Ludicrous? It's the most important piece of history in this entire town! It must be saved."

"It's dangerous. It nearly killed that boy."

Nevaeh was intrigued. What were they talking about? She walked over to another conversation and listened in.

"I hear he's going to die."

"Stop spreading gossip, Mrs. Peabody, he's a strong young boy who's going to be fine."

"How do you know? Are you a doctor?"

"I'm a friend of the family. He's got a broken arm and two broken ribs and a slight concussion. But he's going to wake up soon."

"You can't know that. Nobody knows what's going to happen."

Nevaeh walked towards another group talking and listened to them.

"We need to tear it down."

"It should never have been let stand for as long as it has. It's a danger to us all."

"It's beautiful and historical."

"It's where some boy, maybe spent an afternoon talking about it, and the mayor decided to make a plaque commemorating its existence. It's truly nothing special."

"Nothing special? SOME boy? How can you say that? That tree is the tree the Painter's son talked about. He gave his first lesson about our creator using that tree as his diagram. The insight that young man had was marvelous. How can you possibly disregard that? How could you even contemplate saying that tree is nothing special?"

"Because the story was from generations ago, Dylan. We don't know if it was true."

"Of course it was true." Dylan countered.

"It doesn't matter. It took place so long ago that it isn't at all relevant today. There's no such thing as the Painter – and oh yeah, there's a boy lying in a hospital bed grasping to his life because of it. Anyone who's against tearing down that tree is as insane as the parents who begged everyone to ask Geody to help him."

Nevaeh was completely taken aback. Her father had told her the story about the tree. She saw the painting of it hanging on the wall in his den. She had always wanted to see the tree, to see with her own two eyes, the details he talked so vividly about. When she first arrived in the Painting there was so much to see, so many amazing sights and sounds. She had been overcome with the multitudes of different options, places, people. Her senses were flooded with so much opportunity that she had all but forgotten about really focusing on each and every minute detail. The universe, the world, the town was massive, to her, how could she focus so intently on the details of one little tree when she had seen a billion trees covering miles and miles of landscape across an entire globe.

Of course she had studied the trees. She looked at so many of them over her travels they blended into the environment. Short trees, tall trees, trees wider in circumference than a house. There were trees of various shapes, colors; so many types of leaves, or needles, some bearing fruit, others grew flowers... she never thought she'd ever find the one tree in all of the world that her father spoke so highly of so long ago, and yet, here she was, within walking distance.

"It's got to be torn down."

"It'll destroy the town."

"How could the loss of one tree destroy an entire town? That's preposterous!"

"Because, that tree is the only thing that's kept our town on the map all of these years."

"In case you haven't heard, we've got a great manufacturing company in town. THAT is what has put our small, dying town back on the map, not that overly large, dangerous tree."

"People," a booming voice came from the center of the room. Nevaeh made her way over to see a couple of people standing on stage by a podium. "We can't solve this problem tonight."

"Sure we will – tear down that tree!"

"No!" shouted a huge group of people from every section of the room. "You can't!"

"Watch me!"

"Both sides have valid points. There is a lot to take into consideration for a decision like this and we must go about making that decision in the best, most fair way possible."

The crowd all began to talk at once and Nevaeh's ears hurt from the noise.

"People!" The man spoke again, regaining the crowd's attention. "If anyone, goes near that tree or tries to destroy it, they **will** be arrested."

"Sounds like you've already made your decision. How is that fair?"

"No one has made any decisions. There are too many emotions surrounding this issue and until both sides are heard, in an organized, legal proceeding, we will not make any decisions regarding the fate of that tree. Once both sides have reasonably presented their case and rebuttals, our mayor will make his final decision based on the best possible outcome."

The murmurs and outrage began again, but the town sheriff stepped up to the podium.

"And please let me remind you all, that until the case has been made and the outcome decided, the tree will be under constant protection. If anyone comes near it, intending to cause it damage, defame it, or destroy it, they and anyone helping them, will be put in jail until the resolution of this case. Are we clear?"

Nevaeh was thankful for that. She would hate to see anything happen to that tree, especially before she could really see it in the daylight. She knew this tree was special. It was a historical symbol of her grandfather's love for the Painting, of her father's unsurmountable appreciation of his own father's creation.

While many were just looking at this tree as an obstacle that needed to be taken care of, a danger, it symbolically meant so much more. It was about the people's opinions of Geody. Whether some believed he painted the tree and the world they live in, and the thoughts of other's who couldn't bring themselves to believe. If they got their way, they'd destroy a valuable piece of history, a visual reminder that Geody painted them. But then again, they had the entire world to see that... To Nevaeh, it was about her father, the fact that he was born here, lived here, died here, to teach everyone about Geody's grand plan, about his love for this world. It was the fact that he pointed out that evidence in such vivid detail, one single tree that symbolized such painstaking detail and thought and caring that went into every brush-stroke... THAT was what needed to be remembered.

So instead of heading back home that night, she chose to stay in the Painting. She didn't want to leave until she had seen the resolution. One day in her world was, a year in the Painting. If she went home now, she wouldn't get to see how the peple resolve such a heated conflict. By the time she got back the tree would either still be here or it would be gone and there would be no trace of it having ever existed. She couldn't fathom that.

So she found Dylan, the person who so strongly believed in saving the tree, Geody's love, the man to whom she felt drawn. She followed him home and slept on his couch. Sure, she could have slept outside, nothing could see her, touch her, bother her, but it just didn't seem comfortable. Nevaeh had never slept in anything but her own bed, and she had a feeling she'd be here for quite a while.

The next morning she awoke to the smell of bacon frying, the news blaring on the TV, and her unaware temporary roommate deep in conversation with someone on the phone.

"Yes, I'm going to be the one who speaks for all of Geody. I'm going to need everyone's help to gather as much historical and factual information as I can about the Painter. The other side is going to present this as a simple open and shut case. They're going to say it's an old tree and it must go, simple as that. But our job is going to be much more difficult.

It's our task to prove beyond a reasonable doubt that this should be marked as a historical landmark. That it should be saved, cared for and upheld, because of it's historical significance."

As Nevaeh listened, she realized, maybe she'll be able to help.

Chapter 17

The hustle and bustle of the campaign office was confusing to her. There were dozens of people who filled the room, each at their own desk, either on the phone or computer or both. Some doing research, others calling around for information. She spent weeks watching, listening, admiring these people.

Their goal seemed impossible. While the tree already had significance to it and the mayor had already taken the first step to place the plaque next to it, commemorating its history, it wasn't enough in the eyes of the law.

One person was writing a report about the exceptional value the tree's existence had and what that value does for the town. Another person was in charge of detailing the event that made this tree important, her father's story. A third person was showcasing how the tree represented a great ideal, the existence of Geody, the Painter of the entire universe. A fourth person was detailing the artistic merit with the beauty of this tree, writing down as much detail as they could, trying to recreate Benjamin's speech.

They shared information with each other as well as other researchers, working diligently to combine their data in the simplest most profound way. Their collaboration made Nevaeh's heart soar.

However, on the other side of the room, there was another whole group that was in charge of bringing in conflicting points of view to destroy the first groups research.

At first it seemed counterintuitive, but then Nevaeh realized why they were doing it, so they could be prepared for the debate. They all brought in their own particular pieces of this puzzle, all representing their own sections.

As each side presented their findings Nevaeh sat in awe. The conflict was real, and strong. Each side had such valid points. She could understand where everyone was coming from. Sure, she was partial to saving the tree, it meant more to her than most. After spending multiple afternoons just sitting underneath it, taking in all of its beauty and charm, truly taking the time to understand each detail her father had pointed out, she was filled with a passion for this tree unlike any she had ever experienced before.

She was so happy to be spending time with Dylan, being filled with his hopes and desires. Seeing this world in a way she hadn't taken the time to yet. Sure, she had seen the world, from the top of the mountains to the bottom of the oceans and everything in between, but all she saw was what was there; the final scene. She could marvel at the sunset as it dipped down behind the mountain range, but she hadn't simply looked down at the mountain, the ground she stood on, and taken in the unique topography of the soil.

She had seen fields of green that stretched along prairies so far that they seemed to fade into the sky, but she hadn't taken the time to marvel at a single wildflower, at the exquisite detail of each petal, how the leaves connected to the stems or how the stems were coated with a fuzzy layer of fur to protect it from animals that would want to eat it.

And as she sat under the tree, looking at its limbs that seemed so tired, the thick, weathered trunk, and all of the dead growth just under the canopy of leaves, the balls of moss that had taken over, she realized, Dylan's job was going to be more difficult than anyone had expected.

This tree was tired. It had lived through and seen so much, so many generations, so many lives had come and gone, so many children had grown up around it, left their footprints on its ground and carved their memories on its trunk. Its roots had grown over and around rocks, had come up from under the ground, reached over obstacles and then submerged themselves back under the ground, only to come back up a few feet away and do it all over again. As the roots had been marred by lawn mowers and bicycles and deer horns and scuff marks, new life was starting to sprout from them, attempting to stretch up through the shade of its upper canopy in hopes of finding a ray of sunlight.

It was trying so hard to survive, to endure through the restrictions of its location and the interference from the humans. She saw where tree limbs had been struck down by lightning or broken by weight, where years of drought had slowed its growth, or where floods had rubbed its bark smooth.

Taking the time to really see this tree gave an insight as to why things in this world must live and die. Why buildings come and go, why people have cycles, and that all things must eventually come to an end.

No, she did not want to see anything happen to this tree, for every reason Dylan had brought up and for every emotion she had tied to it, but she also didn't want to see it or any other child suffer under the weight of a broken limb or crumbling structure.

It had been many months. As the debate began, her fears, her worries, her doubt and aspirations filled the arena. She hoped her father and grandfather were rooting for them, watching from afar, filling the people with the ability to be open to see both sides, but only time would tell.

Nevaeh's mother was beside herself. As she stood by her daughter's bedside she held back the tears. "She's been asleep for so long."

She spoke while holding Benjamin's hand. "How long will she be asleep?"

"I don't know." Benjamin voiced honestly after explaining that her presence was living inside of the Painting. He turned to see his father walking into the room. "Is this how you felt, when I was living in the Painting?"

Gerald nodded. He gave Nevaeh's mother a hug to calm her down. "She's going to be fine." He tried to confirm.

"She missed breakfast."

Gerald understood this mother's worry but he knew in his heart that everything would be fine. He just didn't know how to help her understand.

"Wake her up!"

"She will wake up when she is ready."

The pounding of the gavel on the outdoor podium brought the crowd to attention. The entire town, it seemed, had come out to watch. People had brought chairs and blankets, picnic lunches; it seemed they were here for a show. Some had chosen a side, others were here to judge, while others really didn't care about the outcome one way or another.

It was difficult to absorb, but somewhat understandable. If they were unclear of the debate, ambivalent regarding the fate of the tree, or torn whether the child should have even been climbing on it in the first place, they'd all have indecisiveness about them.

Yet, as the moderator of the debate relayed the rules, detailing the necessity for a peaceful assembly and calm from the crowd, Nevaeh was consumed by something else. She could feel the tension building within Dylan.

As he paced under his canopy, with his group of advisors encouraging him, his heart began to race. "I can't do this."

"Of course you can. You are the best chance we have to win."

"We have confidence in you."

"You can do this."

But Nevaeh could feel him doubting himself, fearing what was going to come of this, worrying about what others would say, or think or react to his passionate sureness of Geody's existence and the justification of keeping the tree no matter how the family or others feel.

Nevaeh stood by him. She placed her hand on his shoulder, even though he couldn't feel her. She willed her spirit to fill him with the courage he needed to see this through. "You can do this. I believe in you."

Dylan inhaled deeply, filing himself with the determination and tenacity to stand up for what he believed. Then he began with his opening remarks.

The debate was harsh and filled with emotion. The young child had awakened and was doing better, but his injuries were on-going and the testimony from his parents was moving.

The opposing side asked questions like, what would you have done if your son wouldn't have woken up? What if his injuries would have left him in a coma or paralyzed? The tears running down the mother's face as she contemplated the absolute worse was enough to sway any opinion, but Dylan was great.

"But your son woke up didn't he?"

"He did, thanks to Geody."

"Thank Geody." He smiled brilliantly. "In fact, your son's arm will heal soon, and he's expected to make a wonderful recovery, right?"

"That's right. I want to thank everyone for your well-wishes. It means a great deal to our family to know so many people were thinking about our son during this trying time."

"How do you feel about the tree?"

"I..." she paused, not knowing what to say.

"Do you blame the tree for hurting your son?" Dylan carefully inquired.

"I can't blame the tree, it's not like it was malicious in its attempts to hurt my son."

"Do you blame the city for not tearing the tree down, before anyone got hurt?"

"We love that tree. I've grown up with this tree. My husband and I courted under the tree. We picnicked under it. I looked forward to watching my son climb it."

"Even though it was so old and others worried about its longevity?"

"It has stood the test of time. I figured it would be around for my children and grandchildren, and even their grandchildren."

As they took their first break, Nevaeh was proud of Dylan. She looked at the opposing council and noticed them planning their next move. Curiosity got the better of her and she walked over to listen.

"Is our next witness ready?"

"She just arrived."

"Great." He said as he collected his notes.

An elderly lady slowly made her way up to the podium, she walked with a cane and was very shaky on the ground. After she introduced herself, he began with his questions.

"Can you tell everyone what happened to you in regards to this tree?"

"It was my own fault, really. It was dusk, the landscape lights hadn't come on yet and I was running late for my book club. I decided to cut across the square, and I tripped on one of the tree roots that stick up above the ground."

"That's horrible. What happened?"

"I fell. I fractured my hip bone, twisted my ankle, sprained my wrist and broke my nose."

"That's terrible." Council spoke as the crowd murmured. "But this wasn't your fault, you were walking in a protected park. The Mayor himself is responsible for the upkeep of the area, that tree."

"Well yes, he is, but I probably shouldn't have crossed under the tree. It was too dark to see the roots."

"So the lights hadn't come on yet. If they would have, you may have seen the roots?"

"I would have."

"So, tell me. What did the Mayor offer to do for you?"

"Oh, he was so kind! He felt so badly about the accident that he offered to pay for my hip replacement surgery."

"Oh, that is very generous."

"Yes it is. I certainly can't afford it. The medical bills are piling up." She added.

"So our town is out quite a bit of money because of this tree. Money that could have been saved if he would have just taken down the tree in the first place."

"Well, he did make the lights be on full-time so no matter when it starts to get dark, even during a storm, it will always be well-lit under the canopy of the tree."

"And what if the lights go out? What if someone else gets injured?"

"I-I don't know."

"Wouldn't it make more sense to remove the obstruction, the problem? Would you want this to happen to anyone else? Would you want any other person to get injured like you, go through the pain of a fractured hip bone, broken nose and hip replacement surgery?"

"It is quite painful. I wouldn't wish this pain on anyone."

"Yet, the Mayor won't tear down the tree."

As the day ended and everyone went home, Dylan knew he had his work cut out for him. The trial was only beginning, it seemed, and the town was already starting to turn in favor of tearing down the tree.

He had made many valid points today, but so did the other side. Dylan wasn't sure how he was going to sway everyone's opinions. And that's what would need to happen. He'd have to convince everyone not to tear down the tree. That suddenly seemed like an impossible task.

As he made himself ready for bed, Nevaeh heard him ask Geody for help and guidance. She added to his plea and then wondered if her parents were okay. She had been here for many months already. She knew in her world that wasn't very long but she did know that by now, her mother would be concerned. It was probably after lunch now.

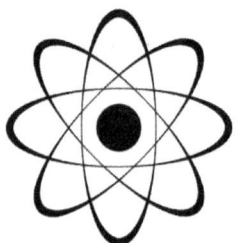

Chapter 18

Sitting next to her daughter's bedside, she glanced over at the stone cold bowl of soup she brought in and wondered how much longer it would be before Nevaeh woke up. How many meals can she miss before she becomes too weak? When should she call in a doctor?

"I remember, as a teen, I went to bed on a Friday evening and woke up on a Sunday morning." Benjamin's words broke the silence. "Yes, I was hungry, but I was fine. Sometimes a little extra sleep is a good thing."

"Yes, but she's not JUST sleeping, is she?" She took her daughter's limp hand into her own. "What is she going through? What is she experiencing? I know you told me about how you lived in the Painting, but I never thought our daughter could get trapped there."

"She's not trapped, she is choosing to stay, to see this through." Gerald spoke up as he walked back into the room. "There is quite a debate going on in this little town. A moral dilemma, and my granddaughter is on the front lines, willing everyone to have heart, to listen and care and give everyone a chance to be heard. It's beautiful."

"But she's alone."

"She's not alone, we're with her in heart."

"She's alone in a huge world, surrounded by strangers who are in conflict." Nevaeh's mom added. "Conflict that can turn into a dangerous battle if the emotions get too high."

"She is perfectly safe," Benjamin added, "she can't be hurt by anyone. They can't see her, hear her, touch her..."

"So she has no one to talk to, to comfort her, to guide her or help her understand what is happening."

"She's a smart young girl." Gerald declared.

"She's a Young girl."

It had been over a week and the debate was getting more heated. They were no closer to a resolution that when they first started.

Since so many stories had been brought to light, the emotions were even more conflicted than before. The other team had made their cases, plural, for the destruction of the tree, and while Dylan had done his best to counter each one of their claims, his dilemma was the fact that saving the tree was more for historical and emotional purposes.

The town was divided. As each day progressed, it seemed to become worse. The division was pulling apart friends, families, co-workers. Anger was building and fears were growing. A team of people had begun round-the-clock vigils at the tree, in order to protect it from groups of people intent on destroying it.

Nevaeh kept trying to calm everyone down, it was her desire to help, to keep the peace, but it wasn't working. She believed harder, felt stronger, desired with everything she had in her and it seemed her spirit was failing. Maybe it was because she was hungry?

But she couldn't wake up now. If she was gone for just an hour to wake up, eat and come back, more than two weeks would have passed. This whole thing could have gotten so out of hand in that time, a war could have broken out. Nevaeh felt the only thing keeping the people's emotions at check, the only thing helping to maintain order, was her desire. When she felt someone's rage increase too much, she'd go to them, fill them with love, desire that they understood and not retaliate.

But she was growing tired. Weak. She was at it constantly, day and night. Even when most were asleep there were some who wanted to take things into their own hands. Trouble-makers who wanted to vandalize, to tear down the tree. Even with the threat of jail time looming overhead, they just wanted this to end. As did Nevaeh. As did Dylan. But if they gave up, who'd be left to fight for this tree?

As dinner time approached, the tears began to flow down her mother's cheeks. Both Nevaeh's mother as well as her grandmother, Tiffany, sat quietly by her bedside. "She looks so weak, so frail." Nevaeh's mother spoke softly.

"Come," Tiffany spoke, standing up from her chair. She offered her daughter-in-law a hand and led her from her granddaughter's room. She glanced back at her husband, Gerald, knowing very well how this felt. She too went through it with her own son, Benjamin. She watched her son sleep for almost a month, and while she tried not to worry, she did.

Sure Gerald had told her Benjamin would be fine, that he would return unharmed, and he did. There were no physical injuries to him and she was grateful for that. Miraculously, his body had survived without nourishment, but then again, Gerald did have this amazing ability, an enchantment to do things, that no one could truly comprehend.

However, a mother not only looks at the physical ailments of her child, she also sees the emotional conflictions. She knew what Benjamin had been through while he was in the Painting. She stayed with him after he returned, she assisted him as he worked through his inner conflicts, his emotions and strife.

Benjamin suffered for years with a feeling of betrayal and distrust. He had been so good and kind, so thoughtful and giving to Gerald's world, and he was hurt by them. He realized in the end why. He understood how his suffering helped others, how it began the healing, but it didn't necessarily help him.

Knowing all of the good he did, the reinforcement of the Painter's plan, he grasped hold of that tightly, but the brain and the heart are two separate things. His heart hurt. And it was his mom, Tiffany, that saw the change in her son after he came back.

As Tiffany and Nevaeh's mom sat down in the living room she attempted to take their minds off of the situation at hand.

"Benjamin used to tell me about the Painting and his friends and adventures. I think one of the hardest things for him to talk about, with me were his parents, the people who raised him and took care of him for so long inside."

Nevaeh's mom listened to Tiffany as she talked, watching her as she shifted in her seat and clasped her hands together.

"I don't think he wanted to hurt my feelings by admitting how much he loved them, but I was so grateful they were there to care for him, to look out after him."

"But my daughter doesn't have that. She can't talk to anyone."

"She is a part of their lives. She may not be able to interact, but they can feel her presence and she can feel their hopes. She is a part of something so much bigger than we can comprehend. She is lucky." Tiffany smiled.

"Lucky? Have you ever been ignored? Completely forgotten about? Have you ever talked and no one heard you? Have you ever needed something and no one knew to help?"

"I have." Gerald spoke as he walked into the room. "As a child I was isolated, lonely. I was misunderstood and ignored. When I wasn't being ignored, or feeling shame and disappointment, I was being bullied by those bigger than I. I wanted nothing more than to escape, to be anywhere else, and that's when I discovered something very important. In the absence of connection, love and belonging, there is always suffering. I didn't want that to be the case any longer. I wanted to create a world of possibilities, filled with my love.

I loved this world, even when it didn't love me. I wanted so much to provide a place that could overflow with my love, that could overlay hurt and fears, and fill everyone with hope and dreams. I wanted to create a place where I and everyone who felt like me, could be included, could learn and could be filled.

My loneliness and my heartache created a world full of possibilities. It gave me an incredible power and that is what I gave my son, and my granddaughter. They have the power to enact change, the potential to transform lives, to change futures and to see and feel and hear and experience this massive potential.

I understand your worry, your fear, but understand that a few missed meals was nothing in the grand scheme of things. Conversation is not the only form of communication. Love can be given in more ways than a hug, and your daughter, my granddaughter, has a power, the spirit, to bind a whole planet together for the good of it."

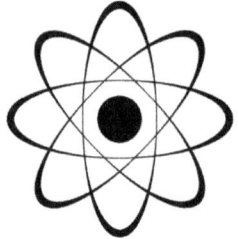

Chapter 19

As the storm clouds rolled in, no one noticed. The emotions were building, so strong, everything was about to burst. People were filled with anger and despair. Squirrels were more agitated, birds had flown away, wolves were howling in the distance, and the wind was picking up, whipping through the town like a rushing bull, charging at its captor.

Nevaeh was crying.

She was going from person to person, helping to smooth things over, willing them to understand, to not take things into their own hands, to not make a decision that would hurt others – but she knew – something had to give. She was standing in a minefield of emotion and the bombs were about to burst.

"People, you are friends, neighbors. You don't want to do this."

A thunder clap startled a child but his parents didn't notice. Lightning off in the distance was blocked by protestors' signs. The people were coming, gathering from every corner of town, culminating in the town square, surrounding the tree.

"Please, everyone. Please don't do this."

Officers and city officials were trying to hold back the angry protestors. Dylan's people were pleading with the people, yelling through a bull horn, beseeching those who would listen to be civil.

"Please hear him. Please calm down."

Nevaeh climbed the tree. She stood at the top of it. She saw the storm rolling in, heard the wind swishing around her, trying to knock her down, trying to defeat her. The thunder rattled her ribcage. The lightning lit up her eyes. The rain was starting and yet, the people kept coming. They were all so angry, ready to fight.

She only had mere moments before they all clashed. Her fears built within her. What was she going to do? How was she going to stop them? They couldn't even hear her! Her desire was peace, it flowed out of her with so much force it drained her of every bit of energy she had and still she persisted.

Someone pulled out an axe. She heard a chainsaw roar to life. She heard a scream.

The chanting and yelling and begging and pleading rose above her into the sky like a flood of hate that was drowning her. Her emotions were piercing her heart, her desire to end this kept growing and growing until it burst from her soul like an explosion in the night. Stomping her foot down with as much force as a child having a terrible temper tantrum she yelled at the top of her voice.

"STOP IT!!!"

At that exact moment a lightning bolt struck the center of the tree. The surge of electricity shot through the limbs and out through the sides. A large crashing sound built into a roaring disturbance that deafened the crowd. And as all turned to see, to acknowledge what was coming, they discovered a terrifying sight. It was too late – the tornado had touched down and it was heading right towards them.

Screams arose as the crowd panicked. Pandemonium filled the streets. The wind was pushing people over, into other people who were losing their footing, feeling as if they were being sucked up, being pulled away. The crowd clamored as confusion filled them.

Dylan barked into the bullhorn, "Get to the school! Help everyone get to the school."

Larger fellows grabbed the arms of smaller fellows, enemies they had been yelling at mere moments ago were now their top priority. They pulled each other close, protected strangers, and they all ran, together, towards the school.

Some people wanted to run the other way, towards their homes or their businesses, but they couldn't. Vehicles were being lifted into the sky and slammed down on the ground in front of them, forcing them to lurch, skid to a stop and turn away. Wind gusts veered around buildings, knocking people backwards, breaking apart fences and throwing the wood fence posts and planks at the crowd. Loose debris rocketed through the air like projectiles, herding the people like cattle, directing them away from the approaching tornado.

People helped people. They offered their hands, they pulled them to safety, they shielded the young with their own bodies. As the tornado closed in, Dylan and his team made sure everyone made it inside of the school. They pulled the doors closed. They held the doors, feeling like they were being pulled out towards the suction of the tornado, they hollered as their feet skid to the threshold, "I can't hold it!" Other larger men ran to the door. They grabbed part of the horizontal handles and pulled with all of their might. They worked together, opposite sides of the fight, coming together for a common good – survival.

Those who were yelling just a few moments ago, ready to start a war, reached for Dylan and pulled him backwards, helping to keep the doors closed. They came together to save each other, to save everyone. Enemies found comfort in each other, they held each other, protected each other.

The roar of the tornado barreled down around them. The air seemed to be sucked from within the gymnasium, women and children were crying, men began pleading for mercy. A child's voice cried out, "Help us, Geody." The words filled everyone's hearts, they all felt it. They all claimed it. "Geody, have mercy." Their hearts were pounding in their chests, the pressure was pounding in their eardrums, their will was strong and combined.

A barrage of hail began clashing against the building. Windows shattered as rain entered the room.

The people's fears merged into one. Their desires to survive, to live another day, blended into one massive request: "Geody, save us!"

Nevaeh had been watching the tornado barrel its way down the street towards the school. She had witnessed the people come together, to help each other. She watched as they all entered the school – the same place she had first met them when she arrived. She felt their faith growing as they helped each other, huddled together and pleaded for salvation.

Nevaeh felt that their desire to survive, all of them, together, was strong. She too desired that the tornado would cease, would relinquish its grip on the school and lift away, and at that exact moment – it did.

As quickly as it had begun, the tornado disappeared. The wind stopped. The debris that was spiraling around in the air, dropped to the ground. The clouds parted and a small ray of light shone down through the dark grey sky and in through the broken window of the school.

The huddled masses slowly looked up from their clusters. They saw the light, the clearing sky. They heard the silence and hesitantly, began to feel that it was safe. They checked on each other. They assisted those that had been injured. They helped the unsteady and weary to their feet, and they walked together, outside, hand-in-hand.

They were quiet.

They slowly made their way down the street, taking in the damage, benches thrown through windows, fence planks sticking out of walls like shot arrows, debris and tree limbs scattered all over the ground. That's when they saw it – the tree.

Or what was left of it.

Chapter 20

As the clouds cleared and the sun shined down on the destruction throughout town, the people surveyed the damage. They all walked up to the tree, the topic of such heated debates and confrontations for so many weeks, and as they gazed upon it, they cried.

The tree had been split down the middle. Its weak, heavy limbs, what was left of them, held up one side of the massive trunk.

Dozens of limbs had been snapped from it, yanked away and discarded throughout town like crumpled up trash. Leaves been plucked from it, leaving so much of it bare, naked, weak looking. What had they done?

This once proud tree, that towered over their town, that symbolized life and love and the determination of Geody to provide for them, had been mangled and destroyed.

The people were heartbroken, ashamed. They held each other and cried. They were happy to have survived, grateful to still be a part of each other's lives, and yet saddened beyond anything they could have ever dreamed.

What had once seemed so important became anything but. Their family, their friends, neighbors – that's what was important. They had spent so much time and hate attacking each other over this tree, hurting each other's feelings, destroying friendships, for what?

They had forgotten how important the people were. Each of them had been out for themselves, their beliefs, their wants and desires. They didn't care what anyone else wanted or said, they refused to listen, to compromise, to try to get along. This tree that was supposed to be symbolic of love and beauty had torn apart a town, and a tornado, of such wild, uncontrollable destruction, had opened their eyes in under a few minutes time.

Had this been Geody's plan? An opportunity to disconnect in order to reconnect?

Nevaeh thought about this for some time as she watched the people of the town. They held each other, shook neighbors' hands, people that had been at odds – so angry – so full of venom, now shyly looking small, apologetic. Without saying the words, many people expressed their apologies through their actions. And then, when no other adult knew what to say, a child spoke for them.

"Mommy, I'm hungry."

Those three words lit up the town.

"The electricity is down."

"It'll be back up soon."

"I don't think so, the power lines are down, scattered across a hundred acres."

"I just got off the phone with the electric company – they've been slammed. Everyone has been redirected to the neighboring town to assist in *their* clean-up efforts. They don't think they'll be able to get to us until late tomorrow or even the next day."

The grocery store manager grimaced. "But our perishables, the milk, the meat?"

"The ice cream!" A child from within the crowd called out.

A few people chuckled, but a point had been made. Thousands of dollars of food was going to go bad. It was going to be a big waste.

A check-out clerk offered a creative suggestion, "Maybe it's time to throw a party. We survived a tornado. We should celebrate – say, with a bar-be-que?"

"Food and fellowship!" An older lady's voice lifted from within the gathering and a few others joined in cheerfully.

"How will we cook it?"

"I've got a grill." One of the men spoke up.

"I've got a camping stove."

"Me too." Other deep voices bellowed back.

"Okay, so we'll gather the perishables and bring them out here. If anyone needs ice to stock their freezers, come and get it while it's still frozen."

"Everyone who can assist, grab your coolers and head down to the grocery store to help. The rest of you go gather anything you have that you can donate to a town festival. We'll need tables, plates and utensils..."

"The church has a bunch of folding tables and chairs, we can set up a picnic area out here... by the tree."

The town all stopped their planning upon being reminded of the tree. They turned to look at what was left. They took in the destruction. Limbs had been ripped from the trunk. Leaves sprayed across the entire field. It looked bare.

But worse yet was the lightning damage. The grand trunk, as thick as three people trying to hug it, had been chopped down the middle. It looked as if it had been pried apart by a clamp, and the insides were charred black. It was actually still smoking just a tad.

As they stared at what remained of the tree, a dead tree with broken limbs and a fractured body, they also remembered Benjamin and how his body had been fractured. They remembered the stories he told about the tree, his father's plan for the world. They were reminded of its promise, the hope they all felt when they had grown up around it.

The sadness began to take over, to consume them. A morbid silence took over the crowd – they shared a moment of silence.

Wow! Nevaeh thought to herself as she observed the people. She felt a tear fill her eye and escape down her cheek. It fell onto the trunk of the tree and splattered on the dark, charred debris.

Then just as suddenly as the quiet hushed them, they were back to planning and scattered to take care of their tasks. Within less than an hour there were over two dozen grills sizzling and smoking. There were hotdogs and hamburgers, grilled chicken, fish and even steak sizzling from all corners of the town square.

There were men, women and children fast at work collecting debris, chain-sawing broken limbs, raking leaves and cleaning up.

Over fifty tables were brought in. Hundreds of chairs and even more coolers were scattered across the grounds. Some of the mothers brought yard games to keep the younger children occupied. Musicians brought their instruments. They set up a makeshift stage across the street to provide a fun musical ambiance. Couples danced. Children laughed.

The people of the town had all come together, in the most miraculous way.

As the sun began to set, ingenuity continued, many people parked their vehicles around the square and flipped on their headlights. The local scouts built a campfire and used the trees downed branches as kindling to keep it going.

Some of the children started talking about making this into a campout. Next thing you knew tents were brought out and setup. Sleeping bags appeared. As many of the children fell asleep, the majority of the adults stayed up talking and socializing throughout the night. The people of the town hadn't done anything like this in decades.

As the morning sun began to rise over the hilltops, the grocery employees brought out the eggs, sausage and bacon. Breakfast aromas wafted into the children's noses, and they awoke from their slumber with giggles and joy.

Milk and orange juice flowed into glasses and cups of coffee were poured. When it seemed most everyone had a cup in their hand, the pastor of the church clanked his glass. As the crowd hushed, glasses were raised to neighbors, to friends and to loved ones. The

Pastor cleared his throat and then took a deep breath. When he spoke, everybody heard him.

"Friends, neighbors, townsfolk, join me as we lift our cups to the sky. A sky that was painted for us by the great Painter Geody. A sky that brings sunshine to warm us, light to guide our way, and a cool breeze on a hot summer's day. The same sky that brings rain that promotes growth and quenches our thirst, also brought the tornado – that brought us together.

We were down. We had knocked each other over with our words and actions. We had nowhere else to go but up – but we couldn't see it. So what happens when life knocks you over? When you're lying on your back, down and out – lost without a way? You look up! Look up to the sky and then find a way to touch it - get up and keep moving forward.

The Painter has given you everything you could ever need to succeed. He's given each of us the tools we require to help those around us. He's given us the knowledge and the common sense to see somebody's hardships, the compassion to acknowledge what they seek, and the love in our heart to assist those who lack. It is us, individually, who choose not to let that happen.

Just remember, you count. You have worth. You have been given the ability to enact change because each of you are significant in Geody's eyes. In each of your hearts, is a desire; a desire to do good. It is one of the most powerful tools you will ever have. It's the engine that ignites our will; the will to make good choices, to do good. We each have to make the decision to open our hearts to the needs of others, to use our judgement to find alternatives, compromises, and work with our fellow man.

We may not understand *why* things happen the way they do. We may not understand *how* things work out. But we all can find ways to understand *who* is in charge. We are no more in control of our lives than a tree is in control of the weather. We are solely dependent upon a higher power, upon each other, upon any number of variables that dictate what is going to happen in our lives.

We have to believe in ourselves. We have to work together to benefit each other as well as mankind. We have to work on it, to focus on our dreams, on our goals. Look at what we accomplished in one short night!

We got it done. We pulled together as a community. We looked out for one another, we shared time and music and food with our fellow man. We broke bread together. We proved to each other that silly arguments, conflicts, and disagreements, can't truly separate us from ourselves unless we let them. We can do anything we put our minds to, if we all work together.

Resolve, right now to keep moving forward, to keep working with one another. Let us establish a covenant of friendship and togetherness by doing FOR others. This is your moment – right here, right now, to appreciate what we have, to welcome our neighbors into our hearts and to thank Geody for the gifts he has bestowed upon us.

Thank you, Geody, for sparing our lives. Thank you for showing us the error in our ways. Thank you for bringing us back together again. Thank you for our friends and family and neighbors and community. Thank you for always showing us the way of good. We appreciate you!"

Chapter 21

The townsfolk cheered, they applauded the pastors speech and they hugged one another. They were happy, satisfied, wanting nothing because they felt complete. And as those feelings washed over a very satisfied Nevaeh, the rumble of trucks rolled into town.

"It's the electric company!"

With the knowledge that the town would be fine, that the people had come together - the hopes for a better future exploding within her heart. Nevaeh decided it was finally time to go home.

When she awoke, she saw that she was surrounded by all of her loved ones. Her Mom and Dad, her Grandparents, they were all sitting by her bedside.

"She's awake!" Gerald proclaimed joyously as Nevaeh slowly started to sit up.

Her mother pulled her into a great big hug as Benjamin hugged his own mother, Tiffany.

"We were so worried about you! You've been asleep for days!" Her mother cried.

"I'm okay Mom. Promise."

"I wasn't sure you'd ever wake up again."

Benjamin glanced over at Gerald who glanced over at Tiffany. They had all been through this, in one way or another.

"Mom, it was wonderful. Horrible and then wonderful." Nevaeh began as she turned to her grandfather to continue explaining.

"They were all so angry, arguing, fighting one another. I wasn't sure how to fix it, if I *could* fix it. It kept getting worse and worse until a storm began to build. The wind picked up and the clouds rushed in and they grew thick and dark. There was such vivid lightning and the thunder was so loud. And all it did was make the already angry townspeople angrier. They grew louder and more vicious, it was breaking my heart. I could see what it was doing to the children. I could feel the hate seething through their veins. I couldn't stand it any longer and I screamed for it all to stop."

"And did it?" Benjamin inquired.

"No!" Nevaeh sat up straight and looked at her father. "A wind storm, a violent funnel-shaped whirlwind poked down through the clouds, touched the ground and began tearing apart the town! It seemed to herd the people together, directing them into one direction. They all ran to safety, huddled up together in a nearby building and they were so afraid. I could feel their fear. It was over-powering, but it was also unifying. It was the first time in weeks that everyone was thinking and feeling the same thing. And do you know what happened when I felt that? When I felt their combined pleas for survival and safety?"

"What?" Her mother asked as she sat on the edge of her seat.

"The tornado dissipated. It dropped all of the debris it had collected and had been throwing around the town, and it just dropped it. It disappeared as fast as it had arrived. And in its wake, it left destruction. It destroyed the thing that had been the cause of all of their conflict, and when they saw what happened they all grieved for it.

"What was it that was causing so much conflict?" Nevaeh's mother inquired.

"Dad's tree."

Benjamin glanced at his daughter. "My tree? What tree?"

"The tree you taught your first lesson on. Your friends, spoke of that first lesson so much, to so many people. They shared the knowledge you gave them about Grampa's grand plan and the town saved that tree. For so long that tree stood and grew. Its limbs were so heavy, it tired of holding them up and when a small child tried climbing those limbs, they collapsed and the child got badly hurt."

"That's horrible." Nevaeh's mother voiced. "Did they cut the tree down?"

"That was the debate. Whether they should or not. The town was divided, half wanted it cut down, half wanted it saved. No one could agree so the tornado made the decision for them."

Nevaeh's head lowered. "What's wrong sweetheart?" Benjamin asked.

"The tree seemed so important. It was a visual representation that my father had been there. So many people shared fond memories of it, looked forward to seeing it, and now they won't be able to. It's so sad."

"What do you mean they won't be able to see it?" Gerald inquired coyly.

"The tornado destroyed it."

"There's nothing left of it at all?"

"Well," she thought, "Most of the limbs had broken off. It had been split down the middle of the trunk by a lightning bolt. Surely they wouldn't keep it in that condition... right? Wouldn't it be dangerous to keep it like that?"

"The people of my Painting can be quite the visionaries when inspiration hits them. Their artistic creativity is enough to marvel the most imaginative mind." Gerald spoke as he stood from his chair. He reached his hand to Nevaeh's hand. As she took his hand, he led her out the door downstairs. "Let me tell you about some of the stories while you have yourself a nice meal."

"I *am* hungry!" Nevaeh rubbed her belly with her free hand. "How long was I asleep?"

Chapter 22

That night Nevaeh couldn't sleep. Of course, she had had plenty of sleep recently to last a while. Still, she stayed up all night listening to stories from her father and grandfather. She truly understood how things worked in the Painting now, and she marveled at how much could change in such a short period of time.

As Benjamin would share stories of life one day at a time, Gerald would share stories of life one call at a time. Nevaeh, however, described the world one moment at a time. Each perspective was distinct and fascinating, but they were each separate. Each viewpoint was expressed in relation to how the other experienced it and Nevaeh realized how neat it would be if they could each share this experience together.

"Wouldn't it be cool if Grampa could see what you saw Daddy, from your perspective from the ground?"

"It would..." Benjamin acknowledged, "and wouldn't it be neat if we could soar through the universe like you had done and see all of your watercolor nebulas up close?"

"It would..." Gerald answered, then turned to Nevaeh "and wouldn't it be nice to feel the whiskers of a soft bunny tickle your nose?"

"Yeah!" Nevaeh agreed with delight. "Can we? Can we?"

"Nyos" Nevaeh heard both men speak alternate letters together.

With confusion, she asked, "Which is it? No or yes?"

"No." Benjamin spoke.

"Yes." Gerald clarified.

Benjamin and Nevaeh both looked at Gerald with wonder. "Yes?"

"Of course." He smiled. "I painted it. You, Benjamin, were born into it, and you gave Nevaeh the gift of visiting it. Of course we can all go there."

"I don't understand, Dad. How? You've never been able to visit it, not since you put the Painting inside of the Universe."

"Nevaeh can take us inside, and you can help us become a part of it."

"How?"

Gerald shook his head with a smile.

After a bit of explanation, which still didn't seem at all feasible, they accepted the possibility. Gerald was so certain as he explained, how could they possibly disagree? The three of them looked at each other with Cheshire smiles on their faces. Nevaeh was eager to show them everything she had seen. Benjamin was curious beyond compare and Gerald was just smiling from ear to ear.

"Will it be safe?" Benjamin inquired.

"I won't let anything happen to her," Gerald placed his palm on his son's shoulder, "or you."

Benjamin felt butterflies swarming in his stomach. He was nervous and excited. He trusted his father more than anything and he loved his daughter more than that. How could he not be worried? But also, how could he not want to go back and share this with his daughter?

This would be the experience of a lifetime.

"When?"

"What better time than the present?" Gerald stood and held out his hands.

So, the three of them stood side by side in front of the universe painting. Standing in the middle, Benjamin took his father's right hand and Nevaeh's left hand and closed his eyes. He thought fondly of the Painting, the world he had loved so much for so long, returning there, being a part of it again. When he heard Nevaeh's shriek of excitement he opened his eyes to see a sight he had never seen before.

"This is the universe Painting!" Nevaeh beamed brightly as she pointed with her free hand at the colorful clouds of watercolor paint she had added to it. "Aren't they beautiful?"

Benjamin marveled at the stars, at the size of the planets, at the nebulas and at the sun. They were shooting through the universe, speeding by so many marvelous sights that he had only seen from an extreme distance spiraling around his father's canvas.

Nevaeh was leading the way. She had seen all of this before, spent weeks observing it, exploring it. She was in a rush to get to her Grampa's world and while disappointed that he wouldn't get to truly spend the time he wanted exploring here, Benjamin was excitedly filled with the knowledge that he could come back any time he wanted.

"Over here!" Nevaeh squealed as she led her father and grandfather towards the most marvelous Painting in all of creation.

As they flew closer to the planet Benjamin heard the sounds of the world. An eruption of noise pierced his ears and he tried to slow them down. The pain was evident on his crinkled face and Nevaeh saw this.

"It's okay, Daddy. The closer we get to town the quieter the rest of the world becomes."

Nevaeh pulled her family through the stratosphere and rushed them through fluffy white clouds. Clouds that Benjamin had only ever seen from the ground – so far away, he was never able to touch them, only dream about.

Watching them pass by, Benjamin looked down at the world, at mountains he had spent days climbing, feeling exhausted at the end of the day. They were flying over them like they were minute drops of paint. They looked so different from this viewpoint. From this angle, looking down at the world was a phenomenon that he had never even dreamed of doing. He knew his father had painted the world, *He* had seen it, but Benjamin never got to see the Painting from his father's perspective. It had long been secured within the universe when Benjamin came along, and growing up within the Painting, was so much different than this experience.

"Do you know where you are going?" Gerald asked Nevaeh, who was leading the charge past cities, prairies, rivers and deserts.

"Of course! It's just past the ocean." Nevaeh giggled as she turned to her dad and caught his eyes. "Remind me to take you there, Daddy. It's so much more than you could ever imagine!" She recalled his stories about fishing and swimming but not being able to hold his breath too long.

As they landed in the town square Nevaeh's eyes beamed with delight as she stared at the scene in front of her. Her father, however, was looking all around at the town. He kind of recognized some things, the buildings surrounding the square were similar, but the businesses had changed. Facades and designs of the architecture had updated the look, but some of the framework was similar.

Gerald watched his son and granddaughter stare at his world in amazement. He heard the birds singing. He felt the wind sweep across his cheeks. He smelled the aroma of the flowers… he felt Nevaeh pull from his hands and race across the street.

Benjamin felt her pull from his hand and he spun his attention to her quickly. She was racing across the street, in the direct path of an oncoming car. "Nevaeh!" he raced to her, sweeping her up into his arms and landing on the opposite side of the street.

"What did you do that for Daddy?"

"You aren't here in spirit today. You are here for real. You can really get hurt if you aren't careful."

"I'm so sorry!" The driver spoke, as he stood out of his vehicle. "She came out of nowhere."

"She's okay. Thanks!" Benjamin voiced back as Gerald made his way across the street to join them.

Benjamin helped Nevaeh back to her feet, and she immediately went to what had attracted her attention initially. "They made benches out of some of the downed tree limbs."

"Those are gorgeous." Gerald smiled.

"Look over here, they've carved animals into these." Nevaeh pointed at them.

"And scenes." Gerald added seeing two baby bear heads poking out of a cave with a momma bear standing watch over them outside. He loved how much time was obviously spent carving these scenes.

Benjamin noticed one that looked like a basket full of food, and a scene of a fishing boat on the water. "Such craftsmanship."

"This one has words carved into it and a design that looks like a paintbrush and palette."

Benjamin and Gerald followed Nevaeh as she scoured the grounds admiring all of the carved artwork.

"Tourists?" Someone spoke, as they walked up to the three. Benjamin looked over at the man surprisingly. "We get a lot of tourists these days – come to see the new tree and the saved artwork."

"What saved artwork?" Gerald asked.

"The carvings of initials and hearts and memories that had been collected on the trunk of the tree over the generations. One of our local artisans carefully carved each off the trunk and made them into decorative pieces of historical artwork that can be seen hanging on the walls of our businesses along the square."

"What a wonderful idea." Gerald smiled.

"New tree?" Nevaeh inquired, wanting to continue exploring but being held there by her father who was holding her hand.

"Not long after the great storm that struck down the tree and brought the townsfolk back together again, one of the local groundskeepers noticed new growth sprouting from the center of the destruction." The nice man led the three to the center of the square and pointed at it.

"A bolt of lightning split that massive trunk right down the middle and burned the center leaving only the outer shell of the tree. Little did we know, that shell provided protection and safety for the new sprout to grow and prosper. So, as you can see, we have a new sapling, the starts of the old tree bringing life to a new tree from within itself."

"It looks like two hands holding it." Nevaeh admired as she noticed how the artisan, after saving the carvings, had carved the remainder of the old trunk into what looked like two large old hands carefully cupped around the new tree sapling.

Benjamin noticed a plaque and leaned in to read it aloud. "The hands of the Painter protecting his children."

Gerald beamed, "What a beautiful representation of old life giving new life."

"It is," the friendly man agreed. They all looked at the tree for a moment and then the man spoke. "I'm Dylan."

Nevaeh's head turned quickly to see the man closer as Benjamin spoke. "I'm Benjamin, this is my father, Gerald."

"Hi," Gerald spoke as he shook Dylan's hand. "This is my son, Benjamin and that spirited young girl is my granddaughter, Nevaeh." Dylan kneeled down to introduce himself to Nevaeh at her level when she ran to him and give him a big hug. Startled, he looked at Gerald and Benjamin in wonder.

Benjamin kneeled down before Nevaeh and spoke, "Do you know Dylan?"

"Dylan is the one who stood up for...." Nevaeh slowed seeing an odd concerning look in her father's eyes. "The big debate... to save the tree? He was the one who led the side to save it."

"Wow! You know your history." He spoke proudly to the young girl. "But there are plenty of people in this world named Dylan..."

"But only one I know who felt so strongly about preserving the past."

Realizing this was the man Nevaeh had followed for months, Benjamin felt even more fascinated. He reached for and shook Dylan's hand again. "Sir, it is an honor to meet the man who stood so strongly to save the tree."

"I had a huge team to help – it wasn't just me." Dylan's cheeks flushed. He knew the story had stretched across the land, but it had been a couple years since someone recognized him as *the* Dylan from the stories.

Over the course of the day Nevaeh showed her father her favorite places in town. Some of them had already changed and her disappointment was apparent but Gerald didn't allow her to stay sad for long.

"Change is important. Growth is key. This world was designed to keep spinning. Motion, advancement, it's the dynamic I painted. I don't want the world to get complacent, to forget. I want them to appreciate this Painting, to explore it, to love it. To see everything..."

"Trust me Dad, that is not easy!" Benjamin spoke. I lived here for over 30 years and hardly scratched the surface."

"Exactly," Gerald added as the three of them walked down the beach. "It's impossible for a single human to experience everything the Painting has to offer – that's why there are so many humans. I gave every single one of them a gift, the gift of creativity. They each have their own unique imagination, a resourcefulness and a drive.

There are musicians who share the sounds and rhythms of the world, and artists who paint or photograph the landscapes we can't go see in person. There are the writers who detail the stories and describe scenarios that other-wise would never have been considered. There are people with disabilities who show us how to appreciate ourselves in all of our strengths or limitations. There are those with little who demonstrate appreciation, and those with more who offer giving. There are people with large families and those with none and so much more.

When I painted this world I focused all of my energy on its beauty, on the nature and plants, the environment and weather. I made sure everything worked in collaboration – even if from the human perspective it seemed like chaos. Storms brought rain for growth, fires provided a clearing for space, and earthquakes designed to shake things up to curb complacency. Everything had a reason, and so do the people.

Every person has a reason to be here - whether it be big or small. Each individual has their own part to play, their own story to live out, their own impact to make. Like ripples in the water, every human's story matters, they are all integral to the grand design. Even when they are no longer visible in this Painting their memories live on, their adventures continue, and they become a legend."

"Wow." Nevaeh expressed as she looked up at her dad to see him nodding his head in understanding, "Grampa, you're amazing!"

Gerald blushed. The three of them were silent as they continued their stroll out onto the pier. As the morning sun began to rise over the shimmering waters of the ocean it reflected the extreme colors in the sky. The pink, red and orange hues faded up into the dark blue as if the night had been a shadow and the universe was being washed away to create a new canvas of possibility.

Nevaeh watched a dolphin leap up out of the water and dive back in, then another. "Can we go see them?"

Benjamin's thoughts went back to his human limitations, that he couldn't hold his breath long underwater, that his arms tired of swimming after a while.

"When we are here on the Painting we can do anything we can imagine," Gerald conveyed, knowing what Benjamin was thinking. "Let's go swim with the dolphins."

"Yeah!" Nevaeh jumped up and down clapping. "And then, Daddy, I can show you the depths you never got to see before."

"That would be wonderful." Benjamin smiled in delight at his spirited young daughter.

"I can't wait to show you how I got to see the world. I'm going to teach you so much!"

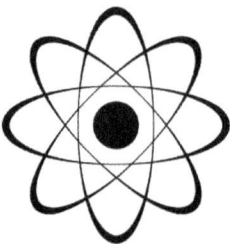

John 14:26 But the advocate, The Holy Spirit, whom the Father will send in my name, will teach you all things and will remind you of everything I have said to you.

Who am I to write this story?

I ended the first book with this question and my answer was basically a dissertation of how I listened to God who led me. I ended the second book with this question and discovered that God likes to test you and your faith.

So I will now, end this book with that question for a third time, and what I've come up with is this: to believe is not enough.

I had my own small confrontation with a tornado one week after writing about it in this book. Watching the destruction first hand, how our heavy, sturdy building was pulled apart by the wind. Staring in awe as fragments lifted into the air and danced around like butterflies, weightless and beautiful. It was terrifying to know that even those small sections were too heavy for me to move by myself during clean-up. It's amazing to realize the power and strength of God.

Why did it happen? Oh I know – I was being taught by a higher power, or those lost loved ones above were looking out for me. It could have been worse – they simply brought to my attention things that needed to be addressed, and I think that's what this book is intended to do.

Your relationship with the Lord may be strong, you may wholeheartedly believe that, but is it really? I consider Him my best friend. I thought I talked with Him all of the time, but I realized I didn't. I neglected our relationship just as much as I neglected my own friends. The term 'being busy' is not an excuse, it is a way of living, and that is not a good thing.

When you are too busy to talk to friends, or even with God, you are making yourself unavailable. It's a good thing God doesn't get too busy for us. *Believe me when I tell you, there is definitely a plan and we will never know what it is, in life.*

The other thing I have noticed, while doing all of this writing and introspection, is that every new scenario in my life brought about new insight. Two weeks after writing about Nevaeh naming the tadpoles frogs (because that's what they will eventually become) I wrote a blog post with an entirely different insight – God doesn't tell us what we're going to grow up to become because He doesn't want us to think we failed Him.

I honestly don't know where this story came from – I mean – I KNOW – but I didn't plan it. How was it, that my life, my trials, my own uneducated insight brought to life a Painting that inspired so much with so little? How did everything tie together so perfectly, without an outline, strategy or agenda? How was it that a name came to me out of nowhere, that when abbreviated, spoke volumes. That when sounded out became the entire theme for the next story, whose soul existence opened the door to a spirited story of goodness? How did I write the biography of the Father, Son and Holy Spirit without even writing a rough draft?

To believe is not enough. I believe we are all here for a reason. I believe that bad things are only bad in our eyes, and I believe that if we never give up on God's plan, He'll never give up on us. I also believe that thinking I believe all of that, even saying it out loud, doesn't truly mean I believe it. I don't think our minds are capable of understanding the depth of love God has for us. I think the best thing we can do, the only thing, is to accept it. To be open to the changes that will come into our lives and look back to find that ah-ha moment.

I cannot even begin to tell you how many times in my life I've looked back after a trial and said, wow, was *that* the plan? How did He know I needed that? It's truly amazing to see how things turn out, but you almost can't ever look back right away and see the reason, that comes later – when you least expect it. You just have to be open enough to see it when He presents it to you. You just have to trust and believe.

Acknowledgements:
To New Friends

To "The Little White Light" who's story of a city come together after their own tornado sparked the inspiration and conclusion to this story. I had been struggling with what would bring people together because we so rarely see it in life. I should have known it was that easy.

To my Grandfather – who recognized the value of simple time spent with one another, not talking, just being. I will never forget those peaceful, musical evenings. It showed me how much could be conveyed without uttering a single word. It's a calm I will seek for the rest of my Earthly life.

God works in mysterious ways.
It's not a cliché if it is true.

About the Author

Kathleen J. Shields is an award-winning author having won First Place Best Educational Children's Series from the Texas Association of Authors for "The Hamilton Troll Adventures".

The Hamilton Troll series is educational and inspirational, teaching young children social skills, animal characteristics and how to handle real-life situations.

While awaiting illustrations, Shields' writes chapter books for her slightly older readers. While still infusing education into each story, Kathleen endeavors to entertain young readers, igniting a desire to read that will span a lifetime.

Shields' also runs a website and graphic design company called Kathleen's Graphics. She designs colorful, eye-catching websites, logos and advertisements for businesses and authors. She enjoys being challenged to learn new things.

Additionally, Kathleen writes an inspirational and educational blog regarding her endeavors as an author as well as a business woman and Christian. Her views are always light-hearted and thought-provoking and are intended to get the reader thinking.

For more information about the author,
and her books, please visit:
www.KathleensBooks.com
or follow her blog at:
www.KathleenJShields.com

More Great Books By this Author

Ghost Dogs

As a toddler Jamie develops an amazing gift, the ability to see Ghost Dogs. They look just like our past pets, just a bit more transparent.

Dream World Defenders

Ryan and his friends enter the dream world where they can do anything they can imagine – the only thing they can't figure out how to do? Wake up.

Constellation Crimes

A Giant Scorpion, a Crab Attack and a Killer Wolf – What do these have in common? The zits on Jared's face! A boys will be boys with active imaginations, story.

Ally Cat, A Tale of Survival

Allison Catsworth gets knocked off of a cliff and instead of falling to her death, she transforms into a cat and lands on all four paws!

A Rainbow of Thanks

Kate walks into a rainbow and is transported to various places on the planet as she tries to get back home. Learn many cultural beliefs about rainbows, also pen pals and paint.

A Rhyme for Everything

A simple play on words from Ecclesiastes 3 There's a time for all sorts of rhyming poems, and all of these have a fun, bouncy rhythm. Inspiration, Greif, Music, Wackiness and more!

The Painting

Gerald is given a blank canvas, so he paints a world, one that he loves so much – it comes to life!

The First Book of a Trilogy

The Painting 2

Benjamin, Gerald's son, decides to go into the Painting to tell everyone about his father, the Painter of their world.

The Second Book of the Trilogy

Dandy Lion, A Legend of Love & Loss

Dandy loses a strand of hair each time he helps someone. He sews the seeds of love by doing good deeds.

The Dog Who Cried Woof

Riley takes it upon himself to announce Daddy's return home, but turns it into a game that goes horribly wrong.

Short Story eBook

Ethan's Reception

FiFi was not happy the day Ethan was brought home from the animal shelter... but Ethan was enthralled!

Short Story eBook

Kathleen J. Shields

Also be sure to check out
The Hamilton Troll Adventures

And for Young Adults:
The Kaitlyn Jones Trilogy

has published various genres of books for numerous authors. Their portfolio consists of a 1200 page Vietnamese to English Dictionary, an award-winning children's series, multiple adult novels and memoires, as well as Christian fiction. Their objective is to promote literacy and education through reading and writing.

www.ErinGoBraghPublishing.com
Canyon Lake, Texas